PETER FAUR

RED METAL

A NOVEL

To Pat, Paul and Kate, who have endured much for me

ONE

Twice a year—once in the spring after the chill vanishes, and again just before it rematerializes in late fall—the CEOs of the world's major mining companies gird for battle, board their Gulfstreams and head toward Teterboro, their metropolitan New York airport of choice, across the Hudson and just 12 miles northwest of midtown Manhattan. Invariably, they travel with a small entourage—a pilot, a co-pilot, a CFO, an investor relations VP, a PR executive (normally the sole woman in the group), and a junior staff member who keeps track of everything from restaurant reservations to thumb drives. They're met by a limo or two, depending on the size of the group, and whisked to the St. Regis, the Waldorf Astoria, the Four Seasons or the Peninsula.

The CEOs drop anywhere from $1,000 to $4,300 or more a night for their suites. In return, they enjoy a bed the size of Montana, a room-service menu featuring $8 Cokes and $65 filets mignons, and at some hotels, a personal butler on call 24 hours a day. Mostly, they want a night of peace and luxurious isolation before their next day's ordeal.

They come for one reason: to run through their PowerPoints at mining-related investor conferences. They get 20 minutes plus a Q&A session to wrestle whiz-kid analysts—often the same age as or younger than their children—into believing the stock of their company is worth buying, and worth buying now. Analyst recommendations have a strong influence on stock price, so winning their favor is an important part of a CEO's job.

Beginning about two weeks in advance, the CEOs' lawyers, advisors and handlers help them work through their spiels and practice answers to any and all questions that might surface. Their real job, though, is to try to coat the CEOs with a temporary veneer of civility. In the cocoon of power surrounding them, CEOs don't often get challenged, and most of them have to be coached to forego the withering looks and tongue lashings they dispense so easily to those summoned to their corner offices.

Some wear their masks better than others. They're the ones who enjoy the game of matching wits with the best, newly minted MBAs from Harvard, Wharton and Columbia.

Others have all they can handle to keep the veneer from cracking. Not far beneath the surface, they resent having to court little pissants who've never had to fight a union, wrangle a price concession from a supplier, or negotiate a decent interest rate from a lender. About a decade ago, one of the pissant haters caught my eye.

I'm David Brown, and I started Galileo Capital Management in the late 1990s. I was 33 at the time. You'd call me a hedge fund manager—and I was—but I'd ask you to believe we're not all cut from the same cloth. Or at least entertain the idea. I wanted the money, of course, and when I started out, I played games like "short and distort." I'd sell a stock short; spread a few, well-placed rumors to create a panic; and make several million when the stock price fell and I bought shares back to cover my position.

That kind of thing works—you see it every day—but eventually I stopped. I might have had a pang of conscience or two. Mainly, though, I figured instead of playing games, I could rake in a lot more money by making sport of CEOs who can't feel the intensifying tremors preparing to shake their world to its foundations. Which is why, in the spring of 2005, I went to the Albright Swanson Mining Investor Conference at the St. Regis to watch Jeff Fowler in action.

Fowler's company, Red Metal Corporation, mined copper, and a lot of it. Three billion pounds a year, to be exact, whenever copper prices turned for the better and its mines revved up to full production. Do the math. Every penny increase in copper price meant $30 million more in sales for Red Metal, and prices had jumped from 70 cents a pound at the end of 2002 to $1.50 in the spring of 2005. That multiplied out to about $2.4 billion a year more in revenue—or a billion and a half in pre-tax earnings—with more to come if copper prices continued to climb (and they did). Red Metal's stock price had more than doubled in two years. Naturally, the company scrambled to turn out every pound of copper it could scrounge from the ground in Arizona, New Mexico, Chile, Peru and Australia.

Fowler's session took place in the Versailles Room, which, true to its name, is all gilt-and-glass chandeliers, plush carpet and drapes, ceiling rings and medallions, velvet flocked wallpaper, and paneled mirrors. It could have been airlifted from France and dropped whole cloth into the second floor at the St. Regis. When I entered, I had my first real look at the man from Arizona.

You'd spot him immediately as a CEO—tall, balding and brawny, more than big enough to dominate the lectern he'd be using, and dressed according to the code of the time, nearly—white shirt, red tie, but in a gray suit a few shades lighter than the usual charcoal gray. New Yorkers would mock it, but it probably withstood the heat better than standard-issue gray in the convection oven that is Phoenix five months a year. Someone had thought to add a nicely patterned, dark-red pocket square for a touch of style.

Fowler made the trip to New York when he had to, but I'd read, besides mining and his family, his only other pursuit was hunting big game in the West. "If I had my way, I'd be happy if I never had to travel anywhere east of Denver," he said in the Forbes profile published when he became CEO in 2000.

Other CEOs used the time before presentations to allow the Albright Swanson session moderators to schmooze them. Fowler couldn't be bothered. He stayed nose down and head down in whatever words or numbers held his attention, warding off any attempts by attendees or moderators to make small talk with him.

He looked up shortly before his time began, perched three feet above us on the podium erected for the event, scanning the room. One moment, he resembled a bald eagle scoping out his prey. The next, he seemed more like a buck making sure he knew whether any predators lurked nearby.

About 80 of us, nearly all men, sat in the rows of padded chairs facing Fowler. I looked fairly fresh because I had popped in just for his session. The others wore dark suits that had wilted and wrinkled during a morning of nonstop sessions. Some held white Styrofoam cups of stale coffee, others rifled through packets of information accumulated from the day's presentations. Opaque shades covered the windows, but the ceiling-mounted projector threw off enough light to make us visible from the dais.

Fowler must have known some attendees, but he acknowledged no one. His eyes caught mine, and he took a few seconds to size me up. I felt I had been tagged and filed away in his brain for future reference.

I don't intimidate easily. I'm a Wharton grad, after all. By comparison, Fowler's alma mater, the University of Arizona, paled in prestige. But I had to admit, he stacked up as a potentially formidable opponent. The Forbes profile said he held degrees in law, accounting, and mineral economics, whatever that was. He'd beaten out mining executives with seven to 10 years' more tenure to become the CEO of Red Metal. And, I knew, he had spit out three investor relations executives in five years. Good ones, too, I thought, but apparently none with enough game to please Fowler.

As I said, these presentations had the sole purpose of convincing analysts why they should buy a stock, and why they should buy it now. Like any other CEO, Fowler blew through the obligatory safe harbor pitch (which boils down to "any forward-looking statements may or may not be bullshit; we don't think we're lying, and we're acting in good faith, but are we deluded? Overly optimistic? Judge for yourself.") Then he cut to the rest of his slides.

He had his material down cold—every number, every phrase, every fact. He had rehearsed so well that, instead of checking his notes, he watched the audience to monitor their reactions. He didn't rush, and he didn't dawdle. He never lapsed into "ums" and "uhs." He stumbled only once, over the word "molybdenum," a metal sometimes found with copper. He even sparked a little laugh when he said, "You know what? Let's just call it 'molly' from here on out."

I'd heard him described as introverted, but that didn't keep him from projecting an authority that conveyed command of his time and space. He might not have enjoyed speaking, but I could tell he demanded perfection of himself. Chances were he demanded it of those around him, which isn't necessarily a good thing for someone who's supposed to be focused on creating a vision and a future for his company.

Fowler made a simple pitch. The worldwide increase in demand for copper, especially from China, meant good things for Red Metal. His company knew the business well. It had been mining copper for all of its 130-year history. Its hard-nosed management kept Red Metal from bankruptcy during the last downturn in copper prices, and the company's conservative management would avoid doing anything reckless with its newfound fortune. The money would be used for four purposes—to invest in existing businesses, improve the quality of its asset base, strengthen the balance sheet, and finally, reward shareholders.

When he finished, one of the whiz kids stepped into the ring with him.

"Jeff, it appears we have a question from our own Mark Hall of Albright Swanson," the moderator said.

Mark couldn't have been more than a year removed from his MBA program. He looked the part. Navy blue suit, highly starched white shirt, red tie, horn-rimmed glasses, neither tall nor short, trim, ramrod erect, a full head of curly hair, and a tilt of the head that made him seem just a bit cocky.

"Mr. Fowler, from time to time, Red Metal is rumored to be in the hunt when another copper-mining company is up for sale, but you never pull the trigger. Companies who make the acquisitions have seen them do well, and these days, with copper prices where they are, it seems you'd have little reason not to be aggressive in buying another company. Will you continue to be as conservative as you have been when it comes to pursuing these opportunities?"

After a smirk he made no attempt to hide, Fowler shook his head and replied: "It's Investor Relations 101 not to comment on any specific opportunities we may or may not be pursuing, as I'm sure you learned in school. I also don't comment on opportunities we may or may not have pursued. Are we conservative? Sure, and thank God we are, or we would never have made it through the last tanking of copper prices. Being conservative, in fact, has gotten us through 130 years.

"You're seeing an extraordinary spike in copper prices, and I'm sure you can think of all kinds of ways for us to spend our new money. But I've been in this business long enough to know the bottom can drop out overnight, and it's damned tough to make it through the hard times. For once, I want to go through the next downturn—and there will be one—with a cushion.

"We'll look at any decent investment, but I'm not going to go on a buying spree just because happy days are here again. Besides, wouldn't it be smarter to hold onto our money and buy later, when company valuations are down again? We understand the business, and we'll manage it for the long haul. We'll share the wealth with our shareholders—we plan to, when it's appropriate. Maybe you'll understand if you stick around a while."

Mark's shoulders sagged, and his eyes fell to the floor. Fowler might have had the short-term satisfaction of chastening him, but if Mark proved to have a long career as a copper analyst, he could strike back in numerous ways in coming years. Not a smart move on Fowler's part, I thought.

The Red Metal CEO took a few more questions, answered them with all the grace of a pro wrestler, and said a quick, perfunctory thanks when the session ended. He left the room with his CFO and Todd Williamson, his investor relations

VP, doing his blocking and tackling. People tried to stop him, but the VP intervened and told anybody with a question to email him, not Fowler. If he could, he'd respond later.

I followed, watching Fowler stride through the hallway and disappear into the elevator. I took a few minutes in the hallway to listen to people react to Fowler's remarks.

"Pretty damned sure of himself."

"Smart guy, for sure. Tactful, no. Smart, yes."

"He doesn't tolerate fools lightly. He seems to think we're mainly fools."

I'd heard enough, so I took the stairs, left the hotel and walked to my office to come to a decision about whether it would be worth investing time and money to take down Jeff Fowler and his old-line, out-of-step company.

TWO

April can be iffy in New York, but that day, the sun shone, flowers bloomed in planters, and the breeze hitting my face smelled unusually fresh. Walkers normally create a current as powerful as the Hudson River rolling toward New York Bay, but they had slowed a step or two to enjoy the crispness of the day. Which frustrated me. I wanted to hurry, and I weaved through them impatiently, like a roller derby jammer trying to get to the front of the pack. Eventually I slipped through and made it to our offices at 405 Lexington Avenue—the Chrysler Building. I wanted to talk with my partner, Gary Gutzler.

Once I decided I needed to be in the hedge-fund business, I called Gary. We'd known each other since our days at Fenwick High School in Oak Park, a Chicago suburb, in the early 1980s. We were an all-boys school back then. The school started accepting girls in 1992.

Gary and I both had our skirmishes with the Dominicans who ran the place, for the usual infractions—a nap in class, a wise crack, a missed homework assignment. Our sophomore year, we played soccer together but otherwise paid no mind to each other. Gary first caught my eye during our junior year in World History, when he told Father Congar the Catholic Church nearly kept the world in the Dark Ages by censuring Galileo.

"Not the finest moment for Dominicans. One of our own turned Galileo over to the Inquisition. But all in all, thank God some enlightened Dominicans, and the Jesuits, were there to bring some intellectual heft to the church," Congar told him. As he spoke, his face turned an angry red. I wasn't sure whether he was getting angry at the church or at Gary for bringing up the subject. His head started to look like something akin to a beet sitting atop a white collar just a tad too tight for comfort.

"Thank God the Masons were there to bring some intellectual heft to the rest of the world," Gary said. Most of the class averted their eyes from Father Congar, doing their best not to crack a smile. I laughed out loud. Gary's insolence, and my appreciation of it, drew us a two-day detention that started a beautiful friendship.

In college, we both majored in finance. I went to Wharton. Gary stayed home to attend the University of Chicago. After graduation, we both ended up on Wall Street, learning our craft from the best and brightest. We knew if we became any good, we'd be widely viewed as sharks and weasels, but we figured the money we'd make would compensate for any ridicule we might suffer and any pangs of conscience we might have. We roomed together in SoHo, took part in our share of debauchery on the weekends, and eventually discovered the money poured in, the ridicule rolled off our backs, and our pangs of conscience never materialized. Good times all around.

We found women to marry, and they turned into women to divorce, and then we found more women to marry, and they turned into more women to divorce. Eventually, we settled into satisfying, childless marriages with beautiful women and good sports who stayed happy enjoying our money while we enjoyed the hunt for more. In the late '90s, our personal lives had fallen into place. It seemed like a good time to get together professionally.

I told Gary we'd learned our shit and should capitalize on our knowledge to make some real money. We should start a hedge fund. He bought in immediately and said we should call it Galileo Capital, in honor of Father Congar and the bond he created between us at Fenwick. And so we did. And if I say so myself, we crushed it. By the time we focused on Fowler and Red Metal, we never really had to work again for the rest of our lives. But we hadn't even turned 40 yet, and what would we do if we didn't work? Sit at home, drink beer, eat chocolates and watch Oprah? Not our thing.

As I walked to the office, I called Gary to check out whether Fowler showed up on CNBC. Sure enough, he made his way to Power Lunch. I missed the program, but Gary filled me in.

"I couldn't tell whether it was the infobabe of the day or knowing hundreds of thousands might be watching, but Fowler came across as halfway human. Of course, the CNBC talking heads are more cheerleaders than critics, so he seemed relaxed.

"His game plan for keeping investors happy is to sound reasonable and in charge—'use our money well, invest in our business, yada yada yada.' But you know what I think? He's sitting on a pile of dough, and he doesn't have a clue what to do with it."

"That's what I saw too. He's deluded himself into thinking he's a great executive for getting Red Metal through the last downturn. But that's not so tough, really. Some layoffs, some delays in capital spending, some underfunding of the pension plan, and you make it through. The tough thing is to have a ton of money in the bank and then try to figure out how to put it to good use.

"Some people see opportunity. Some people see a chance to fail if they make a wrong step. And they can't stand failure. I think Fowler is like that. Tight, controlled, always in charge, lots of bravado. Tough as nails, but he'd never want to be seen as falling on his face. He can't figure out what to do next, and I can't think of two better guys to give him some ideas than you and me.

"Look, Gary, why don't you start looking at ways to buy Red Metal shares under the radar? We can pull the trigger in a matter of days, if we decide it makes sense. Then, if we play our cards right, before long, we'll be sitting in Mr. Fowler's office, giving him the benefit of our wisdom. I'm sure he'd love to listen."

"You mean you'll be sitting in Fowler's office! You're the front man, okay? I'm good with that. When the time comes, you go sit in Fowler's office. I'm the brains in the back office. Let's keep it that way."

I agreed. Gary knew he came up short in the filter department, and he might say the wrong thing at a crucial moment. The good paydays we'd created since forming Galileo kept him happy. He didn't want the limelight.

We'd always worked things that way—me out front, him behind the scenes—and we'd done well. No reason to deviate from our pattern.

The best thing about Gary, and me, too? Our fearlessness. We'd seen some really bad times on Wall Street, like when we lost $60 million in a single day after 9/11. Once the markets reopened, they tumbled so fast we couldn't bail from our airline and insurance stocks in time, and we couldn't move quickly enough to get ourselves short.

I fainted for the first and only time in my life. My knees buckled; my head swirled around like it had been thrown into a washing machine. Gary picked me up off the floor, sat me down, and poured me a glass of water.

"It's just a temporary setback, pal," he said as I sheepishly held my head between my legs. "Nobody sane will blame us for this. You'll give our investors a little pep talk, tell them we'll do what it takes to be ready for the next upswing, and convince them to stick with us till the tide turns our way again."

He called it right. Within a month, we came back pretty much whole. Gary and I both came out more confident and much more trusting of the upside that comes after the downside.

Fowler looked like a different kind of cat, more like someone who grew up in the Depression (he didn't, of course) and always expected the worst. That key difference—optimist versus pessimist—would give us a leg up in the battles ahead.

One other difference gave us an advantage. In our pursuit of Red Metal, Fowler would be the hunted, not the hunter. He might escape our traps, of course. He might walk into them. Or he might be spooked enough to make a foolish move to bring his world crashing down without a lot of help from us.

THREE

Before Gary and I set our plan in motion, just to make sure we hadn't missed anything, we gave ourselves a crash course in copper economics. I knew the basics of commodities from my Wharton days, but I'd spent my career trading stocks, so I had a lot to learn. I knew Red Metal had been hauling in a shitload of money. I wanted to make sure I understood why, and I wanted to be confident the money would keep rolling in for the foreseeable future.

So I sat down in front of my computer to do my homework, comfortable in my mesh Aeron chair and fueled by cup after cup of Starbucks Grande Americano. None of those frou-frou drinks for me. My admin, Beth, had a knack for knowing just when to head downstairs for a refill and get a fresh cup in my hand. When I'm in warrior mode, I down about a grande's worth every 90 minutes.

Like most commodities, copper has a way of taking people on a roller coaster ride. Some investors call it Dr. Copper. They think copper has a Ph.D. in economics because it's so good at forecasting economic trends. If copper prices are rising, demand is up, so everything from home and office building to appliance and auto manufacturing to electronics production is making a comeback, or so the theory goes. Usually, if you factor out the froth churned up by the short-term activity of commodity speculators, the theory stands up, and copper prices' ups and downs are a good leading indicator of where the world economy is headed.

The modern hunger for copper began in the late 1800s. It's an efficient conductor of electricity. It's malleable, so it can be formed into pipe and wire. And it's affordable when compared with metals like gold that also can do its job. When America and the world began electrifying their homes, offices and appliances, they created a copper boom. As time went by, when they ran out of money and their economies stalled, they created a copper bust. And so it went through most of the 20th century. In the bust cycles, companies curtailed their mines or closed down production. Companies "furloughed" miners, who found ways to eke out an existence until the next boom materialized and they could return to mining. (Fowler wanted to smooth out this pattern by keeping money in the bank to get through the next bust more easily.)

Technologically, U.S. copper-mining companies had an easy go of it early on. Back in the late 1800s, the ore in a mine like Arizona's Morenci contained something like 20 percent copper, and it took little effort to extract the metal from the ore. Over the decades, as miners pulled more and more ore from the earth, the copper content fell dramatically. Today, Morenci produces ore with a copper content of about 0.4 percent. In other words, 1,000 pounds of ore must be mined to produce four pounds of copper.

To stay operating, the industry had to mechanize both mining and extraction. Underground mining gave way to open-pit mining. King-Kong-sized shovels and haul trucks made it possible to mine hundreds of thousands of tons of ore a day. Smelters and extraction facilities grew in both size and number to handle the needs of Big Mining.[1] The capital investment took billions of dollars, but the industry made it all work. And then it exported its expertise to nations like Peru, Australia, the Democratic Republic of the Congo and Chile, which is now the world's largest copper producer.

For decades, mining companies also have been based in countries other than the United States. By 2005, several of these companies had stepped up aggressively to change the mining landscape. Megamining companies based in Australia and London had become suppliers of a whole range of metals other than copper. Iron, zinc, gold and platinum might all be pouring out of just one company. These companies usually had CEOs who came out of accounting and finance, not mining operations. They treated mines and mining companies like stocks in a portfolio. They'd buy some, sell some, and hold onto the ones best able to make money.

As a U.S.-based, medium-sized company specializing in one metal, analysts considered Red Metal to be unusual in the industry. To Gary and me, "unusual" spelled opportunity. We believed Red Metal couldn't continue to exist in its present state. It probably would have to eat up some other companies or be eaten up itself, and that meant we would have some major leverage in a showdown with Fowler. CEOs don't like giving up the reins of power, and we might be able to convince him we could make good on a threat to wrest the reins from his hands. In his changing world, Fowler had three options— make some smart acquisitions to get bigger; return gobs of money to shareholders through large dividends or stock

---

[1] Many U.S. smelters have closed because of the pollution problems they caused. Today, countries like China, India and Russia—where money matters more than clean air—have more smelters.

buybacks, thereby shedding the cash that made his company an acquisition target); or do nothing and hope to go unnoticed. Truth be told, Number Three wouldn't work in the real world, so Fowler had only two options if he wanted to keep sitting in his corner office.

I also had to convince myself the upward trend in copper prices would continue for the foreseeable future. Obviously, as cautiously as Fowler played his hand, he didn't count on it.

For most of the late '90s, copper had held steady in the range of about $1.10 to $1.20 a pound. Then in 1999, the bottom dropped out. For the next three years, copper producers like Red Metal had to deal with prices as low as 70 cents a pound, and they started hemorrhaging money. Then, along came China.

For about 20 years, China had been pouring money into its coastal cities, and it created some of the world's most spectacular buildings. Each of them fueled demand for copper, of course, and China also had to invest in infrastructure for electricity.

By the early 2000s, the country had poured billions into its coastal cities. But they weren't the whole story. Inland cities like Wuhan also had grown rapidly, but China hadn't built them out like the megacities of Beijing and Shanghai. China contains more than 160 cities with populations of a million or more, and most of them were—and are—works in progress.

The country started tackling its inland infrastructure, and as a result, in 2002, it surpassed the United States as the primary consumer of copper. In 2003, it gobbled up 20 percent of the world's copper production, and demand kept growing year after year.

Red Metal certainly had benefited from China's appetite for copper, but as he looked at the future, Fowler apparently couldn't convince himself the good times would continue. In fact, in its own attempt at hedging, Red Metal had put in place a system of "copper collars," a series of calls and puts that locked in portions of its production to be sold at a profit but at below-market prices. The company believed the collars provided protection against sudden downward swings in copper prices by guaranteeing a price that still would cover costs and produce a profit. But with the collars in place, Red Metal had lost out on multimillions in profits because of its timidity. That seemed predictable, I thought, but it mattered not to Fowler and his board. They seemed more concerned with staying in the black and putting cash in the bank than in maximizing profits. Oceans of money still rolled in, but the company left behind millions and millions of dollars.

Fowler had much more experience in the copper industry than I did, but I decided his experience, coupled with his apparently cautious nature, hindered him. I sensed the upside of a copper super cycle that would continue for years to come. I had to be right, because I planned to place the biggest bet Galileo ever made on my assessment. I rose from my desk and headed for Gary's office. He'd been doing his research as well, but he needed a break, so he and the *Ghostbusters* pinball machine he kept in his office had entered a tussling match with one another. Good thing the building management had soundproofed our walls. I waited to talk until the ball whizzed past his flippers and fell between them into the trough of failure.

"So, Gary, what do you think? Has Fowler got it right? Is there any reason to believe copper is going to tank sometime soon?"

"Man, my guess is if he owns a bike, he's still using training wheels! You have to believe China's going to be gobbling up as much copper as it can get its hands on for five years, maybe longer, and you can't just fire up new copper mines overnight.

Increased demand, not a lot of increase in supply. There's only one way copper prices can go, Dave, and it's not down. I say we give ourselves the gift of Red Metal shares, and lots of them."

"I'm with you. Do what you need to do to get us to 5 percent. No reason to be sneaky about it. Do it slowly enough so we don't drive up the stock price faster than it's going already. But when we get there, no reason to ask the SEC for a confidentiality period. I want Mr. Fowler to know we're one of his biggest shareholders. This guy doesn't seem to listen to many people, but like it or not, he's going to have to listen to us."

FOUR

By mid-June 2005, we reached an ownership level of five percent, and we had to file the SEC documents revealing our new status as big-time owners of Red Metal. We made quite a splash in the news that day. Galileo had a reputation on Wall Street. About three years earlier, we had forced the sale of Mangelsdorf Pharmaceuticals to Leibrecht Smythe Barnes. Mangelsdorf stock had languished for years, even though it had strong product lines and a promising pipeline. In a euphemism Gary and I think we coined, we saw the company as "undermanaged." We took a large position in Mangelsdorf and then actively courted Leibrecht to buy the company.

We made a simple pitch. Mangelsdorf had good products, but it lacked skill in managing the FDA approval process, and it left too much money on the table because of archaic contracts and a hopelessly old-fashioned marketing organization. Leibrecht already knew Mangelsdorf had a great pipeline and solid products. We convinced the Leibrecht CEO he could extract a lot more profit using Leibrecht's superior management skills. (What CEO wouldn't buy that line?) We also told him Leibrecht could get products out of the Mangelsdorf pipeline more quickly than the Mangelsdorf management could. Leibrecht bought Mangelsdorf at a 35 percent premium, and we brought in nearly $350 million for our investors, a much smaller group back then.

The Mangelsdorf deal made headlines, it made our name on Wall Street, and it made a lot of people flock to our doors. In the beginning, we had to do many a song and dance to get people to trust us with a few million. After Mangelsdorf, everyone who was anyone wanted in.

Anyway, when we self-identified as major holders of Red Metal stock, everybody believed we had unspoken plans for the company. Within 15 minutes of the SEC filing, my Blackberry showed the number of Jim Stevenson, a Bloomberg reporter.

"So, David, I see Galileo has taken a significant position in Red Metal. You just enamored with the stock, or do you have some hijinks in store?"

"Jim, we're major shareholders now, so we believe in the stock. You don't hold five percent of any company unless you think it's going somewhere, right?"

"Sure, but the question is, is it going somewhere on its own steam, or is it going somewhere because you're going to give it a nudge or two along the way?"

"C'mon, Jim. You can look at the numbers yourself. This stock has been supercharged the last couple of years. It hasn't needed any help from us."

"Yeah, but I've seen you guys strap on a booster rocket to other stocks, and they've headed into the stratosphere. Same game plan this time?"

"Look, Jim, you know we're all about creating shareholder value, and extracting full value for ourselves and our fellow shareholders wherever we can. Nothing's changed. But that's all I have to say right now. If I have more, you'll be the first to know."

"Okay. Play your cards close to your vest, but please react to something. I talked to the Red Metal IR guy in Phoenix. He said he had no comment on your position, but he'd be watching to see what you might be up to. Are you up to anything, and should he be worried?"

"We're all about creating shareholder value for our investors, right? That should be what Red Metal is all about too, right? As long as we're on the same page, we should be able to live together in the same ocean—or the same open pit, I suppose. Maybe you ought to ask how they're planning to use all that cash to deliver shareholder value now that we're on board. You write that story, and I'll read it."

The truth is, I've never found Bloomberg reporters to be all that sophisticated. They get lost easily in anything having to do with numbers, which is a drawback for a financial reporter. But it's true, so I try not to bog them down with anything more than a few simple concepts. The intricacies of finance and financial statements are beyond the grasp of most of them.

By the end of the day, Jim filed his story: "In the face of the announcement today that Galileo Capital now owns five percent of its stock, Red Metal Inc. said it had no comment and reiterated it has four priorities for the cash being generated by the boom in copper prices—invest in existing businesses, improve the quality of its asset base, strengthen its balance sheet, and finally, reward shareholders."

Then the company dropped a bombshell. Red Metal planned to pay out a special, one-time dividend of $5 at the end of August.

"A Red Metal spokesperson called it right and natural to grant the dividend to loyal shareholders who deserve to participate in the company's good fortunes. He denied Galileo Capital's actions in any way inspired the decision to grant the dividend."

Well, I thought, it's a start. For Galileo and our 10 million shares, the dividend meant a quick $50 million. Not a bad pay day, but not enough. Fowler and Red Metal had to learn a lesson. Galileo now stood as Red Metal's major shareholder, and we expected us and our fellow shareholders to be first among equals when it came to handing out the Red Metal pot of money. I thought Red Metal might be starting to get it but needed a few more lessons before the message sank in.

FIVE

Gary and I lay low for a couple of months. Red Metal stock kept climbing along with copper prices, and cash kept rolling in to the company. The phrase "embarrassment of riches" seemed to be coined just for Red Metal and Jeff Fowler.

After the special dividend, the company hiked its regular dividend from $1 to $1.50 a year. A 50 percent jump probably sounded dramatic to Fowler's ears, but it failed to impress Gary and me. I wanted to confront him at the Schuster Mining Investor Conference in October, but he didn't show.

As November rolled into New York, winter bore down early. We'd already had our first snow, and temperatures had dipped below 25 degrees on two occasions.

One Saturday morning, when I woke up, Shannon had perched herself to look out our bedroom window toward the Central Park Reservoir. Dirty, trampled snow ringed the reservoir, left behind by runners chased off by the frigid air. Her breath fogged the window. Her naked body fogged my brain.

For sure, Galileo Capital helped me get into our penthouse at Fifth Avenue and 86th Street, just a couple of blocks south of Frank Lloyd Wright's Guggenheim Museum. That's a big deal for me, having grown up in Oak Park, which contains 25 homes designed by Wright, including one for himself and his family. At 3,000 square feet, our penthouse measured twice as big as my boyhood home. At $10 million, it cost 20 times as much as my dad made during his entire life as a meat cutter.

My mom is a widow now. She comes to New York a couple of times a year. She tells me it's good to see how the other half lives, good to see I'm the other half, and good to keep company with the other half whenever she can.

Galileo itself had nothing to do with my landing Shannon. We married about the time Gary and I were starting the fund. But let's face it. Charming and handsome as I may be, it was the money I'd made on Wall Street that got me invited to the weekend party in the Hamptons where we met. And the overwhelming success of Galileo—along with my charm and handsomeness—helped keep her interested, I think.

Like me, Shannon grew up as an only child. Her mom died from complications after childbirth. Her dad never remarried, and he died when his plane fell into the ocean during a trans-Atlantic flight, making Shannon the sole heir to the Harrison Chemicals fortune. She didn't need my money, and she wanted to make sure the man she married didn't need hers. I fit the bill. I was doing extremely well when I met her. And later, it didn't hurt that my previous wives and I divorced before Gary and I generated serious dough with Galileo. Shannon came with a built-in bonus. She set Gary up with her friend, Jessica, and before you knew it, we all walked down the aisle together in a double-wedding ceremony in—where else?—the Hamptons.

As she stood by the window, she slowly pressed her breasts against the glass and slightly arched her back. I admired her nicely displayed, shapely ass and her dimples of Venus, those finely carved indentations on her back. As I wondered how long she could stand the cold, she shivered.

That little quiver really got my juices flowing. I gasped just a bit, and she heard me.

"Come here."

I quickly stripped off my boxers, walked over, and wrapped my arms around her waist. I wanted to take her from behind, but she turned toward me.

"I need you to warm these up," she said, pulling my head down and rubbing my face into her ice-cold breasts. I obliged, kissing her already hard nipples. Before long, we fell to the floor. She climbed on top of me, gyrating and using my pubic bone to get herself off. We'd just made love the night before, so I easily held back until she finished. When I came, I exploded.

We spent a few minutes recuperating in each other's arms. I've always liked lying close together, breathing in the air she exhales. It's one of the little things that makes me feel one with her.

She broke the silence. "It's just crazy cold, Dave, and I'm already tired of it. Let's get out of New York for a few days."

Usually, we'd head for Florida or Puerto Rico. This time, I had another idea.

"How about we ask Gary and Jessica to take a trip with us to Arizona? I hear the golf is great, the shopping is spectacular, and the food is out of this world. We should stay at the Phoenician. The savings-and-loan sharks poured their money into it in the '80s. It's supposed to be one of the most palatial resorts in the world."

"Arizona? I had something closer to home in mind. Florida. Bermuda. Something we know."

"C'mon. It's about time we saw some cactus! And the Grand Canyon. And besides, while we're out there, I can have some fun dropping in on Red Metal and shaking 'em up a bit."

Five days later, Gary and I gave some instructions to the next in command at Galileo—which amounted to letting us know if anything looked out of kilter with the stock market, copper, or Red Metal—and we took our wives by limo to Teterboro to head for Phoenix. We'd never splurged on a corporate jet, but a few years earlier we did the next best thing and signed up with Netjets. For this trip, we chose one of the company's Cessna Citation Encores. It seated seven in large, luxurious, beige, leather seats. The four of us could stretch out a bit. Netjets is so much better than first class, and what the hell, it only cost a few thousand more per body. We thought our bodies were worth it.

As a major investor in several companies, I've been invited on corporate jets from time to time, and Netjets service is as good as anything I've seen on a company plane. When we boarded at Teterboro, we encountered a full selection of anything we'd want to read—Forbes, the Times, the Journal, the New Yorker, and even Cosmo and Entertainment Weekly. We let Jessica and Shannon select the movie, and they wanted to see Wedding Crashers. They'd already seen it, but they told us they thought we'd get a good laugh out of Vince Vaughn and Owen Wilson. We watched it during our meal, which I'd call modest by Netjets standards—chicken breast and a chef salad with vinegar and oil. The women, as always, wanted to watch their weight.

Afterward, Gary and I kibitzed about the Vaughn and Wilson characters. Which of us more nearly resembled Vaughn, and which resembled Wilson? We came to no conclusions. We admired them both for their scheming and their gift of gab. Truth is, though, we thought if you could meld their scheming ways with Bradley Cooper's looks, you'd really have something.

Four-and-a-half-hours after we left Teterboro, we touched down at Cutter Aviation in Phoenix. We picked up two hours flying west, so we arrived early afternoon—76 degrees and, of course, dry. The resort had a limo waiting for us—really nice ride. A stretch Lincoln town car. Clean, late-model, fine leather seats, and a well-stocked bar.

"Where'd you fly in from?" our driver asked. "New York, huh? I don't blame you for coming our way. It looked cold as hell on TV!"

He called himself Mike, a stocky fellow with a scruffy beard and a smile as big as Times Square. He'd spent his early years in Niagara Falls. His parents moved to Phoenix shortly after he turned eight. They'd done well in the carpet business in New York, but the Niagara Falls economy had slowed to a crawl.

"They got tired of turning into Popsicles every winter, so they decided to head west and open a carpet store in Phoenix. Did damn well, too, until Pops picked up a bad gambling habit. The debt piled up, and he faced a constant squeeze from the carpet distributors and the loan sharks. He lost the business, Mom threw him out, and my sisters and I have been hustling ever since. Coulda been the carpet king of Phoenix. Now I'm just a pickup artist."

"You must meet some interesting folks in your line of work," Gary said.

"Yeah, lots of people come to party in Phoenix, especially in the winter. Halle Berry sat right where you're sitting now. Her bodyguard sat next to her. Big guy. You wouldn't want to fool with him. She's diabetic, and her blood sugar had tanked when I picked her up. She had me stop at a Circle K and run inside to get her an orange juice. I dropped them at the Biltmore. She got out. The bodyguard leaned over the front seat and gave me a $100 tip. I might have saved her life, he said.

"Jack Hanna qualifies as the weirdest passenger I ever had. Nice guy, kinda flaky, just like he is on TV. Wore the same khaki outfit and jungle hat you always see him in. He and his wife had a baby komodo dragon with them. In a plastic container, of all things! Hanna showed me all the permits, wanted to make sure I knew he was legal. Then he asked if he could put the dragon up front on the seat next to me. Weirded me out, but I said sure. Turns out he was drugged—the dragon, I mean, not Hanna—so I never heard a peep out of him. Hanna said the Phoenix Zoo had signed up to be the dragon's permanent home. Hanna stayed at the Royal Palms. Pretty good tipper, too. $50."

"You get the high-end business types riding with you?"

"Most of the people who make real money here do it in real estate, and yeah, I drive a lot of them around. One thing we don't have a lot of is big company headquarters. Only a handful—Avnet, InSight, PetSmart, Red Metal, and a couple of others. Pet Smart used to be Pets Mart, then some marketing genius got the idea that PetSmart sounded more socially aware, I guess."

"Interesting, but tell me about Red Metal. I have a couple of friends who work there," I lied. "You ever carry Dave Braxton or Larry Alexander?"

"Truth is, I don't remember most of their names. I've taken the head guy, Jeff Fowler, to the airport several times. Cutter, same as yours. Silent type, not friendly at all. Just gets in the back seat, opens his briefcase and digs into whatever papers he's carrying. I barely get a nod when I let him out.

"The other guys, though, they talk when I pick them up. Not to me, necessarily, but to each other when they're traveling together. And they usually have a few choice comments about Fowler."

"Like what?"

"Like the last time I picked up some of the Red Metal guys, they'd just flown up with him to Montana. Apparently he has some of kind of test or ritual he puts his junior execs through. Takes 'em hunting to see how they react and how good they are. Didn't sound social, more like an ordeal they went through.

"Neither of them brought back anything. Fowler, though, shot himself a bighorn sheep and put the head down right in the middle of the aisle of that big old company Gulfstream he flies around in. Just laid down a big piece of plastic and plopped the head down. He told them to watch where they stepped, and if they messed up the head, they could walk back to Phoenix.

"They say he has a list of animals he wants to kill, and he's about 75 percent done. There's an outfit called the Grand Slam Club, and you can be in their hall of fame if you kill all 29 of the big-game animals in North America. Fowler's gunning for that. I'm no vegetarian, but you know, that seems a little much to me."

"Yeah, me too. But what do you think, Mike? Do people like working there?"

"Lately, they'd be crazy not to! Have you seen the price of copper? Bonuses are going through the roof. But, you know, I have a couple of friends who work there, rank-and-file types. They say it's like wearing a straitjacket. Their bosses go nuts if there's a typo or a misplaced comma in their reports. That kind of attitude starts at the top, don't you think? I'd last about a day there, I guess. Too boxed in for my blood."

When we reached the Phoenician, I tipped Mike $150.

"There's Halle, there's Hanna, and now there's Brown," I said. "I got more from the ride than you know. Thanks!"

Mike whistled. "Much appreciated. Very much appreciated." He handed me his card. "If you need a lift while you're here, give me a call. I'll come running."

SIX

That afternoon—Thursday—we just lounged around the pool. Gary and I sneaked an occasional look at each other's bikinied wives. Arizona looked good on them! We both agreed to turn off our Blackberries and just enjoy lazing around for a few hours. Then we had an early dinner and went to bed. Ten o'clock Phoenix time clocked in as midnight New York time, so our bodies told us to get some rest. Before zonking out, though, I left a voice mail message for Todd Williamson, Red Metal's investor relations VP.

"Todd, this is David Brown at Galileo Capital. I'm in Phoenix for a few days and wanted to see whether we could get together Monday. You probably know we own a good chunk of Red Metal now, and I thought it might be a good idea to get to know each other. Looking forward to talking with you. You can reach me on my Blackberry at 212.222.2121."

The next morning, Gary, Jessica, Shannon and I craved breakfast, and we wanted to see what else Phoenix had to offer. We called Mike.

"You need to go just up Camelback Road to the Royal Palms," Mike advised when he picked us up. "I told you Jack Hanna stayed there. It's also President Bush's choice when he comes to town. I hear the Secret Service thinks it's easy to guard. There's only one way in, and it backs up against Camelback Mountain, so it would be hard to make a sneak attack. The restaurant is T. Cook's. Light, airy, comfortable, and the lemon-ricotta flapjacks are to die for!"

"And what if I'm watching my weight?" Shannon asked.

"Not exactly my strong suit! But I'm sure they'll have something really good for you. This is Phoenix. We get beautiful young women here all the time who eat like birds. But not often as beautiful as you two, I might add!" Shannon and Jessica smiled. I made a mental note to add $25 to whatever I ended up tipping him for treating them right.

It took less than five minutes to get there. I told Mike to stay nearby and just start a tab for us. As I left the limo, my Blackberry rang.

"Hello."

"Mr. Brown?"

"Yes."

"This is Susan Findlay. I'm Jeff Fowler's admin. He heard you've come to Phoenix. He'd like to invite you and your wife, if she's with you, to dinner tomorrow night. Are you available?"

Whoa! This took some quick calculating. Gutsy salvo on his part. Was I ready to see him? Did I want to see him?

"Susan, I really appreciate the offer. I'm just about to have breakfast with my wife. We'd thought about going to Sedona tomorrow, but let me see whether I can change her mind. I'll call you back in an hour or so, if that's all right."

Once the host seated us, I took a look at the menu. This might be Phoenix, but we hadn't escaped New York prices. Twelve bucks for a small bowl of berries. Flown in overnight from the Elysian Fields, I guessed.

We placed our orders, and conversation quickly turned to Fowler's invitation. Gary spoke first.

"What do you have to gain? We know all we need to know about this guy. He's cautious, old school, and he'd just as soon shoot guys like us as have a meal together."

"Maybe, but he won't shoot Shannon and me over dinner. And what do I have to lose? If nothing else, I'm sure the food will be outstanding. What do you think he's really up to?"

"Who knows? I'd be surprised if he takes people to dinner often. He obviously knows about us, and he's curious. My guess is he wants to know what we're planning for our piece of Red Metal."

"Which is bigger than his own holdings in the company. I'm just as curious to know what he's planning, but I doubt he'll say anything beyond the usual patter. He doesn't strike me as a guy who will stray one bit from the SEC regs, so he's not going to tell me anything we don't already know. Shannon, you're a big part of this. Do you want to go, or not?"

"Spend a Saturday evening with a tight-ass CEO and his tight-ass wife? When we could be checking out the club scene in Phoenix? Not exactly a great use of time. But hey, Dave, this is your rodeo. If you want me there, I'll go."

"If we don't go, Fowler will feed on it. He'll think I'm afraid or weak. Maybe I call her back and ask whether all four of us could go. What do you think?"

Gary looked like he'd swallowed a bottle of castor oil. "Hey, pal, that's a nonstarter. You're the front guy, I hide out in the office. That's our formula, and I'm not game to change the rules now."

So, after breakfast, I called Susan Findlay and told her Shannon and I would love to join Mr. Fowler and his wife for dinner.

"Great!" she said. "He'll be pleased. I'll make reservations at Durant's for seven tomorrow evening. His wife's name is Janis. How about yours?"

"Shannon."

"OK, thanks. Have a great dinner!"

We used Friday and Saturday to navigate the highs and lows of Phoenix. The high for us? The Heard Museum, which features Native American culture. Its pride and joy is its collection of Kachina dolls, which Hopi Indians use to teach their children about the spirit messengers of the universe. Barry Goldwater donated many of the Heard's dolls. His spirit still seems to be kicking around Arizona too.

The low? Taliesin West, which saddened me as a fan of Frank Lloyd Wright. Compared with the beautiful work he did in the East and the Midwest, Taliesin West looked like summer camp—leaky roofs, cracked paint, lots of disrepair. Give me his home in Oak Park or the Guggenheim over that curiosity any day. If I lived in Phoenix, I thought, I'd want to do something about it.

Saturday evening, we left Gary and Jessica to their canoodling when Mike picked us up. Twenty minutes later, we arrived at Durant's, which has been serving up giant steaks and generous pours of bourbon since 1950. Mike drove over Camelback and down Central then took us around to the back.

"Do this right," he said. "If you live here, you know to go in the back door. You get to see the kitchen, and Lord, the smells! You'll be salivating as soon as you walk in."

We entered about five minutes early, but the Fowlers had beaten us to the restaurant. They had chosen a spot near the back, and they'd settled into the right side of a plush, upholstered, red vinyl, wraparound booth. The maître d' walked us there, and Fowler rose as we approached. I knew he had played offensive line at Arizona. I kept myself in good shape, but next to him, my soccer body looked insubstantial.

He and his wife had dressed like natives, which is to say they already had pulled out their winter wardrobe. Dark blue, wool suit for him, and a beautiful sweater/skirt combination for her. If you live in Phoenix, I'm told, any time temperatures dip below 70 or so, you're cold, and you break out your warm clothes.

Shannon and I looked like the tourists we were. We hadn't planned for anything fancy during our trip. We couldn't pull off anything more than business casual. A blue blazer and khakis for me—no tie—and a yellow blouse and white pants for Shannon. We definitely looked decked out for summer, which it felt like to us. Fowler's eyes lingered on Shannon just a bit too long for my liking, but he conducted himself more graciously than I expected. At 54, he could have passed for mid 40s. Janis also had held up well. I'd read they'd been married for more than 20 years. He definitely had me beat on the marriage-stability index.

"What're you drinking?" he asked us both. He had made it about halfway through a Manhattan. I went with Chivas on the rocks; Shannon chose Silver Oak cabernet. Then he said he felt as though we'd met before. I told him I didn't believe so, but I failed to mention the once-over he had given me at the St. Regis. No sense jogging his memory if he couldn't quite retrieve the details.

"So tell us about yourselves," Janis said. "Where do you live in New York? What do you do for fun? I love the city, but it's hard to get Jeff to go back very often." She spoke with more than a hint of a New York accent.

"I take it you're not from around these parts, ma'am," I said in my faux western drawl. "How'd you end up with a man from Arizona?"

She laughed, the polite kind you do when you're humoring someone. She said Red Metal kept a small office in New York City to deal with international trade matters. Fowler spent a couple of years there as the house lawyer in the early '80s. Janis taught at PS 51 in Hell's Kitchen. She knew a secretary in Fowler's office who set them up. Before Fowler shipped back to Arizona, he asked Janis to marry him. The wedding took place at her parents' church, St. John's Lutheran on Staten Island. That explained how she could even consider leaving New York City. Hell, Staten Island still had farms during her childhood! She wasn't a Manhattanite, which meant she wasn't a true New Yorker, which meant she could entertain the idea that some form of civilization existed west of the Hudson.

"Jeff isn't the most touchy-feely guy you'll ever meet, but he's taken good care of me and our kids. There's been a lot more good than bad over the years. And I've gotten used to the West. It's beautiful, but I still like to see some greenery and a good Broadway play every once in a while."

"I lived in Hell's Kitchen during my stint in New York," Fowler said. "My salary looked skimpy by New York standards, but I could afford a place in Hell's Kitchen. I figured if I had to spend time in hell, I might as well be close to the kitchen. Which reminds me, I saw you two knew enough to come in through the back door here. Quite an operation!"

I told him about our savvy limo driver and said Mike had taken Fowler to the airport several times.

"I know exactly who you mean. He probably told you I'm not the friendliest of passengers. He doesn't know it, but

I ask for him. He doesn't bother me. He knows the fastest route to the airport, and he's good at what he does. He made the cut the second time he drove me. He remembered that the first time, I asked him to go through the Starbucks drive-thru and order a grande iced coffee for me. The second time he picked me up, he had one waiting. He paid attention. He impressed me. But don't let him know. I don't believe in letting people get cocky."

Our waiter came for our order. Fowler took charge of the wine, ordering a whole bottle of Shannon's Silver Oak. He tried to contain himself as Shannon said she just wanted an entrée-sized spinach salad, but he couldn't help saying when you're in the West, at Durant's, you really ought to eat beef. Shannon held her ground. I fared better in his eyes with my order of a 12-ounce filet mignon—medium rare—and a baked potato with butter and sour cream. He ordered for both himself and Janis—a medium, 14-ounce New York strip and an eight-ounce serving of prime rib plus two baked potatoes. Janis seemed perfectly happy to defer to him; they obviously had done this many times before. The waiter left to place our order.

We spent the next hour or so talking about nothing in particular as we enjoyed our meal. Janis and Shannon carried most of the conversation. The most useful information I picked up? It turned out Fowler grew up south of Phoenix in Casa Grande, and his father worked as a cotton broker, which meant Fowler had always been around commodity businesses and knew the ups and downs of having to be a price taker, not a price maker. His dad always made a point of putting aside money during good years, he said, so his family would be able to weather the times when cotton prices sank.

I had no idea Arizona had cotton farmers, so Fowler gave me a quick lesson on the five C's of the state economy—copper, cotton, cattle, citrus and climate (shorthand for tourism). Then, over coffee, he got down to business.

"It's not every day I invite someone to dinner, David. Frankly, being around people wears me out. I don't have the patience for it. But I've been going over in my mind what you might be up to, and I haven't landed on any idea I like. So I invited you here to ask you straight out: What are you up to?"

"Pretty simple. You're all about copper, but really, we're both interested in the sixth C—cash. Honestly, I don't know much about mining and metals, but I have some pretty sophisticated researchers in my office who spotted Red Metal months ago." (Gary and me, but he didn't need to know the details.) We saw the run-up in your stock, but we concluded you still had a good ways to go, so we bought in. We've been happy, but that's changing."

"We're up about 10 percent since I heard about your stake. Not bad, but for guys like you, it's probably chicken feed."

"Okay, let me ask you a question. Your stock price has done extraordinarily well, but your bank account looks even better. You're sitting on a couple billion dollars, even after your special dividend. Sooner or later—and probably sooner—you have to do something with the money, put it to better use than just gathering dust in a bank somewhere. You don't have much patience with people. I don't have much patience with letting my money sitting idle—and it is my money. So what are you going to do with it?"

Now, he slipped into the Fowler glare I saw at the St. Regis.

"Look, the shareholders I know are quite happy with where they are and with how we're treating them. In any event, you know I can't tell you anything other than what we tell the world. We're going to invest in existing businesses, improve the quality of our asset base, strengthen our balance sheet..."

"And finally, reward shareholders," I interrupted. "I've read the copy and heard it so many times I can say it in my sleep. I've seen you do some of these things, but you've done nothing but hit singles, and you have a big bat now. I'm looking to see you hit a home run, and if you can't, then throw lots of money to us shareholders, where it belongs."

"Oh, for God's sake. You have one group of people to keep happy—your investors. Red Metal has to look out for a lot of people—employees, creditors, communities, nonprofit groups who depend on us. And I'll bet you've never even seen a mine to get some idea what kind of capital investment we need. You think it's simple. There's lots of money in Red Metal, and now it's time to give it to you. Hell! You've been involved with the company for less than a year. Well, I've been part of actually running the company for a long time, and I've been around long enough to know today's boom times are tomorrow's busts. I'm not about to get caught short when the next downturn comes. You'll get your fair share, but the board decides what that is, not you."

"Listen, you've choked off millions and millions of dollars with your copper collars. What a waste! If I chose to do so, I could file a shareholder lawsuit for that reason alone. You've got to face it. Either do something smart—and something big—or even those shareholders you're chummy with are going to want your head. Loosen up the purse strings, or make a smart deal! It is that simple."

I could see by the veins popping out of his neck, Fowler might lose it at any second. Me? I wanted to pull my wallet out to make sure my health insurance hadn't expired. He could easily have put me in the hospital with a swing or two. We sat quietly fuming for a while, and then Janis broke the silence.

"Jeff, it seems to me David could use a little education about the copper business, and even if you don't agree, David, I think everyone should see a copper mine at least once in their lives. It's quite an experience. Why don't you two call a truce, and, Jeff, you should take David over to Mordecai to see what it takes to run a real copper mine."

"I'm not sure there's much you can teach him," Fowler grunted. "And like I said, I don't have much patience for people, especially greedy know-it-alls."

There's those great shareholder relations skills on display, I thought. Janis scooted closer to him, taking his hand under the table. Shannon took it as a cue to move closer to me.

"I think it's a good idea, honey, if Jeff is willing. I know Janis and I both would like to leave on a better note than this. What do you say?"

"Well, he hasn't offered the tour."

"If I offered it, would you go?"

"Yes."

"If you were an employee, I'd fire you. If you were an environmentalist, I'd ignore you. But you're a shareholder, so I'll give you your due. If you want to see a mine, meet me Monday at 7 a.m. at Deer Valley Airport, and I'll take you to Mordecai."

"Deer Valley? Not Cutter?"

"No, Deer Valley is where I keep my private plane. I'll fly us over to Mordecai myself. Make sure you wear close-toed, leather shoes. We'll give you the safety gear you need."

Janis then volunteered to take care of Shannon while Fowler and I went off to Mordecai. "I heard you had considered going to Sedona. We have a place up there. Let's go up for a day, and I'll show you around." Under the circumstances,

Shannon couldn't refuse. Gary and Jessica would be fine with being on their own.

At 9 o'clock, Mike came for Shannon and me. We gave him a quick recap of the evening.

"I'll need you to take me to Deer Valley Monday morning, bright and early."

"Not a problem. I didn't know Fowler has a pilot's license, and I doubt many people do. He's a private guy. Tell you one thing, though. He's parking at the right airport. There's some really high-class crates up there. You should be traveling in style."

SEVEN

Fowler stood waiting for me when I showed up at Deer Valley. He'd done all the preflight checks on his Piper Seminole, which, I learned later, probably set him back a cool half million or so. His nicely appointed model came equipped with dual controls that could be used for training pilots. Janis had no interest in flying, but Fowler said he figured his kids might want to learn someday. He directed me to the student seat but told me to keep my hands off the controls.

He lifted us into the air, ignoring me, speaking to the control tower when he had to, keeping an eye on the altimeter, and tracking God knows what else on the dashboard.

We didn't say much on the way over to the Mordecai mine, which, by air, lay about 90 minutes from Phoenix in the southeastern part of the state, south of the gigantic Morenci mine and near the New Mexico border. I didn't want to distract or rile him at the controls, so I kept quiet. He seemed intent on flying, and he said nothing. Until he pointed out what had to be the mother of all hellholes below us—the San Carlos Apache Indian Reservation.

"That was Geronimo's tribe. I've never been able to make any sense out of them," he said. "Most people we deal with are pretty simple to read. Some are outraged about mining. It tears up the land, pollutes the water, poisons the air, whatever. The truth is, mining is more environmentally responsible than ever. I've learned the best thing with people like that is to just let them vent until they run out of steam. They make a lot of noise, and they might even get themselves a lot of press coverage, but when they see they're not having any effect, they move on as long as we don't stir up the hornet's nest.

"Most people we run into are just greedy. How much are you willing to pay for my land? How much beyond that are you willing to pay? How much will you give to my charity if I play ball? How much, how much, how much. That's where you are. How much money is Red Metal willing to turn over to you? That's your question. But you know what? I might get pissed off about it, but at least I understand your game. We're just working out dollars, and sooner or later, we can land on a figure that will work for both of us. Usually.

"But these San Carlos Apaches, they're a different breed. It seems like they act out of spite. We wanted to buy water rights from them about a decade ago. They wouldn't talk to us, even though they have far more water than they need for the tribe, and they could have made good money selling us the rights. And then they got mad when we bought water from another tribe. It's like they felt they could push us around by not talking to us. They fed their egos, I guess, but they cheated themselves and their tribe out of a windfall sitting there for the taking. Weird people. Hell, Red Metal never captured Geronimo. No sense holding it against us."

I couldn't believe the desolate patch of land I saw contained any water at all. It must have been tucked away somewhere else on the reservation.

Before we landed, Fowler gave me an aerial tour of Mordecai. It covered about 20 square miles, so it measured about a third as big as Morenci. But it had everything you'd want to see in a modern copper mine, Fowler said.

"I want you to look around the perimeter of the mine. See all those houses? There's also a grocery store, a department store, a bowling alley, a movie theater, a gas station, a grade school and a high school, everything a town needs. It's all run by Red Metal. We employ about 870 people here."

Counting family members, he said, that's a town of about 3,600 people, which isn't big enough for a Costco to give a damn. Copper doesn't often do the courtesy of being found near urban areas, so if you're going to get people to work a mine, you have to provide what they need to have a decent quality of life. Schools in company towns are especially good; mine managers don't want their kids to suffer a bad education just because they live in the middle of nowhere, so Red Metal paid good money to keep good teachers in mining-town schools.

The Mordecai airport consisted of nothing more than a landing strip, a windsock and a shack with a bathroom and a couple of old timers drinking coffee in rocking chairs. To my surprise, they lit up when Fowler walked through the door.

"Mr. Fowler, good to see you!"

"Good to see you too, Pete. How've you been, Gene? How's the hunting?"

"Haven't been out much yet. But I won a tag in the elk lottery, so I'm going out the week after Thanksgiving. Wish me luck!"

About then a white Ford F-150 pulled up to the shack. A tall, lanky fellow with weather-beaten skin, a few years older than me, jumped out from the driver's seat and came in. Fowler reinstalled his glare.

"Where've you been, Robertson? I told you I'd land at 8:30. I expect you to be here. I don't have time to be waiting on you."

"Sir, it is 8:30 by my watch."

"Yeah, so I arrived a couple of minutes early. You need to plan for that."

"Yes, sir."

"David, this is Bruce Robertson. He's our mine manager at Mordecai. I've asked him to show you around. I have some other things to attend to. Robertson, don't tell him anything not on the public record, understand?"

We rode in near silence to the mine, and Fowler disappeared into an office once we arrived. Bruce sat me down in a conference room and proceeded to show me a 10-minute safety video.

The biggest surprise in the video? If you're driving in an open-pit mine, you keep your vehicle on the left side of the road. Haul trucks in mines are as big as a two-story house, and the operator sits in a cab on the left side of the truck. If he made a right turn from the right lane, he couldn't see whatever might have wandered off to his right, and he might crush a truck, or worse yet, a miner. Making a right turn from the left side gives him visibility to see whatever is to his right. And if a haul truck is driving on the left side, everybody else needs to be too.

Bruce made me take a short quiz to verify I'd paid attention to the video. I passed. He then outfitted me with a yellow hard hat, safety glasses, ear plugs and an orange vest.

"Why's your helmet white and mine yellow?"

He smiled. "It helps us spot the newbies. It's really for your own protection. If something would happen, we'd spot you fast and make sure you get escorted to safety."

As we headed to the mine, Bruce told me he was a third-generation Red Metal employee, and he knew some fourth-generation people. Apparently, if you grow up in a mining town, it gets in your blood. He had two brothers, both mining engineers. More women had come into mining, he said, but it's really a guy's industry. Where else, as an adult, do you get to play with big toys in a big sandbox all day?

Like his brothers, Bruce studied to be a mining engineer. He grew up in Arizona, but Red Metal had sent him to several mines in Chile and Peru. He quit for a while to join an Australian mining company, so he'd also spent time in the Outback. Red Metal asked him to return, made him a solid offer, and he'd been back on the Red Metal payroll for about three years.

"It's family to me. My grandfather worked here, my father worked here, and my wife's dad and granddad worked here too. I'd be proud to see our kids work for Red Metal. It's not just a company. It's a way of life."

"So how does a guy like Jeff Fowler get to be CEO? His father was a cotton broker. He sure didn't come up through the system."

"I'm no expert on Jeff Fowler, and honestly, I don't think of those senior management guys as real miners. He had the tools and the skills to get where he needed, I guess.

"I have a friend in the Phoenix office who said, years ago, he traveled on business with Fowler, and even then he planned to be CEO. Within 12 years, he made it. My friend says he's never met anyone more single-minded or driven.

"I can tell you about a decade ago, when Fowler served as general counsel, we had a companywide strike. He and the other senior managers came here to help keep the mine running. I hadn't been with the company long, not far removed from wearing your yellow helmet at the time. But I drew a salary and didn't belong to the union. So I got to work side by side with him.

"He worked at the concentrator. I'll show it to you on the tour. He asked question after question, but he never had to ask twice. By the time the strike ended, he had mastered that job and ran a shovel like an old hand. He's intense, but he's the sharpest guy I've ever met."

We headed first to repair and maintenance so I could stand next to a haul truck. The tires loomed over me, twice as tall, and they cost about $25,000 apiece. You could fit a small house into the bed of the truck. The Caterpillar trucks used at Red Metal could carry 280 tons, and today there are trucks that carry nearly 500 tons. Forget about fuel efficiency. They burn about three gallons of diesel for every mile they cover.

Next, we went to the edge of one of the pits. He'd timed it so I could see a blast. I heard it, but I really didn't see much. If a blast shoots a bunch of rock into the air, it turns out, the explosives haven't been placed correctly. The point of a blast is to loosen as much underground rock as possible, and if rock is flying upward, the energy from the blast hasn't been distributed properly.

We worked our way down into the pit, which Bruce estimated at about 2,300 feet deep, nearly a mile wide and almost as long. Because pits are always changing, he said, the haul road we took would be gone in six months. Efficiency in a pit is measured by how fast and deep you can expand it, so the contours of the pit are always changing.

Looking up from the bottom, the pit was some kind of beautiful. Really. I knew the concrete canyons of Chicago and New York, with skyscrapers as walls, as well as anyone. The pit struck me as another kind of manmade canyon. It couldn't begin to rival the beauty of the Empire State Building or the Chrysler Building, and it certainly couldn't begin to compare to the Grand Canyon. But still, to think people could make something happen on such a mind-boggling scale both inspired and humbled me. The priests back at Fenwick would be proud. I had a kind of spiritual moment. I wondered whether Fowler ever felt that way about his mines.

We drove back out of the pit so Bruce could show me what happens to the ore. On the way to the processing areas, several bighorn sheep grazed on a hill at the mine's perimeter. It just proves nature and mining can co-exist, Bruce said. I could only think the sheep needed to avoid encountering Fowler with a rifle in hand.

It turns out there are two major kinds of ore—oxide and sulfide—and Mordecai had them both. They go through different kinds of processing.

Regardless of the ore type, the rock from the pit has to be crushed into small particles, and the waste rock gets separated from the copper-bearing ore. How they tell the difference is beyond me.

The oxide ore all gets thrown into a big pile—something called a heap leach pad—and Mordecai's must have been 300 feet tall. Workers douse the heap with highly diluted sulfuric acid, which picks up copper in solution as it travels to the bottom of the heap. It comes out as the darkest, deepest, richest, most beautiful blue liquid I've ever seen. From there, it's pumped into tanks half the size of an Olympic swimming pool. Stainless steel plates are dropped into the tanks, and direct-current electricity is constantly shot through the solution. Over about a week's time, the plates attract copper to form what Bruce called copper cathodes, which are 99.99 percent pure copper and weigh anywhere from 100 to 350 pounds. The whole process is called solution extraction/ electrowinning, or SX/EW for short.

The sulfide ore goes through a series of crushers and mills that turn it into a slurry something like wet sand on a beach. The slurry gets mixed with various chemical reagents that coat the copper particles, and then another liquid called a frother is added. This concoction gets pumped into rectangular tanks, and air is shot into the slurry to create bubbles that float to the top and overflow the tanks.

The chemicals make copper particles cling to the bubbles, which are collected in troughs. When enough is collected, water and liquids are drained off, and copper concentrate is left behind. The concentrate contains about 25 percent to 35 percent copper, which gets sent away from Mordecai for smelting and refining. I had to admit, making money from copper requires large-scale operations and a lot of money and machines.

"So what actually happens to all the copper you mine here?" I asked. "How does it get to market? Who buys it? How does it get distributed?"

Bruce said the copper industry breaks into two big categories, producers and fabricators. Producers mine, smelt and refine, and Red Metal did all three. Fabricators include wire mills, brass mills and foundries.

Red Metal's copper, whether it came from the SX/EW process or from smelting, ultimately had to be made into cathodes with a purity of 99.99 percent. The cathodes normally get converted into copper rod, which is 5/16 of an inch in diameter and serves as feedstock for the fabricators. Red Metal had its own rod mills and also sold cathode to rod mills owned by other companies.

Red Metal sold directly to only about 75 fabricators. The company sold the rest of its copper to warehouses approved by the London Metal Exchange, which in turn usually sells it to fabricators either under contract or on a spot basis. There are more than 700 such warehouses worldwide.

The London Metal Exchange and its Asian counterpart, the Shanghai Metal Exchange, set copper prices worldwide based on supply and demand. They also provide a variety of strategies to help companies manage the risk of the ups and downs of the copper market. As I said earlier, Red Metal took advantage of these strategies, but in doing so, left millions of dollars on the table.

Bruce took me back to the repair and maintenance shop for lunch. Workers brought their own food, but Bruce made sure his admin had box lunches on the table for both of us.

The miners surprised me with their friendliness. I must have looked out of place to them—a sweater-and-khaki, wingtip-wearing city dweller among their denim and work boots. I thought I looked pretty fit; they might have seen me as being on the scrawny side. But they gladly talked about their work and anything I wanted to ask. Which, of course, mainly revolved around what they thought of Jeff Fowler.

"We don't spend a lot of time with him," one of them said, and the others broke out laughing. "But I'll tell you this. He comes here every couple of years for what he calls town-hall meetings, and he makes sure to visit with all three shifts. He does the same at all the mines in North and South America, and he does them all at once over the course of a couple of weeks, so he's gotta be damned tired by the time he's done. He's come through twice now in five years, so he looks like he's committed to doing it.

"I've seen other guys like him say you can ask anything about the business, but most of them have learned to dance around the tough questions. Not Fowler. I've never seen him back away from the facts, good or bad. Even if the company is cutting benefits or laying people off. And I appreciate it."

Another fellow chimed in. "Early on after he started running the company, we had a guy get electrocuted at the SX/EW plant in a freak accident. The main circuit breaker tripped, and it caused a power outage. This guy came in—his name was Brad—and squatted in front of the breaker to check it out. He opened a panel door, and he stuck a metal wrench in a bad place. Ugly sights, ugly smells, ugly sounds. We all fell dumbstruck, and the supervisors sent us home. Brad lived, but only for a day. Turned out the supplier hadn't installed some of the equipment properly, and the way his wrench made contact shouldn't have been possible.

"Anyway, Fowler heard about it within minutes, and he came as fast as he could to visit with the family. Spent a lot of time with them, too. He stood next to Brad's wife when the hospital called to say he died.

"About a month later, Fowler sent out a letter companywide saying he never wanted to have to face a grieving family again because of an accident that happened at Red Metal. And today, there's not a day—not a minute really—where we don't focus on safety. He drives it. I'd say he's a maniac about it. But it's not a bad thing. It's a whole lot better than if he treated a death or injury here or there as part of the cost of doing business."

Later, Bruce returned Fowler and me to the airport for our trip back to Phoenix. I noticed an electric billboard at the entrance to the property. It displayed the current, per-pound price of copper.

"Yeah, in a copper-mining town, we follow the price of copper like I imagine New Yorkers follow Yankee scores," Bruce said. I'm a Cubs fan first, then a Mets fan, but I got the point. "There's not a man, woman or child in Mordecai who doesn't know what copper is selling for. Our well-being—and sometimes our livelihoods—depends on it."

We arrived to an empty airport. Pete and Gene had left a light on for us.

"I hope you got some idea of what it's like to run a mining business," Fowler said. "It's a whole lot different from sitting in a skyscraper pushing numbers around on a spreadsheet, right?"

Just when my views about him started to soften, he decided to piss me off again.

"Look, I see you have to keep a lot of balls in the air to make a company like this work. But as an owner, I expect you to do that, and do it well. You guys push dirt around, and I push numbers. But never forget, there's power in numbers. And as you said, I'm just looking for mine to get bigger. That's still the game."

"I have lots of people to keep happy, including lots of investors more reasonable than you. Frankly, I'm disappointed. I thought you'd prove to be more sophisticated than the wet-behind-the-ears crowd that comes out to play Twenty Questions when I go to New York. You're just like them."

"Except they only have their jobs to worry about. I have millions plowed into this company, and I expect to get millions more back. And you know what? If you treated them better, and paid more attention to your shareholders, you might get a more receptive ear to your thoughts about how your company should be run."

"Most shareholders are happy with seeing their stock double in a short time, and with their sizable special dividends. I'm not sure what your problem is. I guess we'll both just have to keep doing what we do and let the chips fall where they may. I'll promise you one thing, though. This company has been around for 130 years, and I'm not about to let it sink or disappear on my watch."

"You have two options then. Make it grow, or share the wealth with your owners. Anything else, and Red Metal could be tomorrow's Arthur Andersen or Studebaker or Sperry Rand. Just a memory."

We flew back in silence. Just for good measure, before we took off, I made sure the door on my side closed tightly and the seat belt attached firmly to the floor of the plane. Fowler probably wouldn't want to precipitate an unfortunate accident that led to my demise, but as I learned at Mordecai, you can't be too safe.

I'd called ahead, so Mike had the limo waiting for me when we landed at 5. I told him I felt tired but Shannon, Gary and Jessica would probably want to party, so pick some place lively but not too much so. He took us to the Rhythm Room on Indian School Road. It looked seedy from the outside, but the blues bands sucked us all in, and the drinks kept on coming.

The next morning, Mike shuttled us back to Cutter Aviation. I saved his best tip for last—$500.

"For money like this, I'd be glad to be your driver in Manhattan."

"Trust me, Mike, it'll go a lot further here. As long as you don't have too many breakfasts at the Royal Palms."

By this time, I felt I could open myself up to Mike a bit more. As Shannon, Gary and Jessica headed into the terminal, I told him what Gary and I did for a living, and I explained our real game with Red Metal. I asked him to keep his eyes open and to give me a call if he heard anything that might interest me.

"Will do," he said. "You guys treat me so much better than Fowler. I'll be glad to help."

With that, I said my goodbyes and let Netjets take me and the whole Galileo gang back to Teterboro.

EIGHT

During the flight, while Gary and Jessica napped, Shannon told me about her day with Janis. The trip to Sedona began when Janis arrived at the Phoenician about 7:30 in a white Cadillac Escalade and insisted they stop for breakfast at the Vincent Market Bistro on Camelback.

Vincent Guerithault, Janis told Shannon, is one of Phoenix's premier chefs. In 2003, his restaurant, Vincent on Camelback, placed 24th on the World's Top 50 Restaurants list compiled by the British-based Restaurant Magazine. You could easily run up a tab of $300 or more a person by indulging in excellent French cuisine and a few, pricey bottles of wine. But as part of her insider's tour, Janis took Shannon to the Bistro, a relatively inexpensive spot frequented by in-the-know Phoenicians.

The Bistro sits behind Vincent's main restaurant, shielded from the heavy traffic on Camelback. Shannon said the Bistro reminded her of the street cafés of Paris. A wrought-iron fence and a collection of tall, potted plants separated the Bistro from the driveway west of it. The fence protected several outdoor tables, and seating for about 30 more people lay behind two picture windows. Inside, the subtle lighting, mustard-colored walls, exposed roof beams and French countryside furniture gave the Bistro a casual, comfortable feel.

Both women had a light breakfast of almond croissants, jam and coffee. Vincent made an appearance at their table, Shannon said, and he and Janis talked on and on like old friends. Mainly, they talked about the Phoenix Zoo.

It turned out Janis served on the board at the zoo, and Vincent had agreed several times to be the celebrity chef for fund-raising events. Janis told Shannon afterward both she and Fowler strongly supported the zoo.

"Seems odd," I said, "when Fowler's favorite thing in life is killing animals. From what I know, good zoos are all about conservation and species preservation. I don't think they have much in common with big-game hunters."

Shannon said she made the same observation to Janis, although I'm sure she did it with more finesse than I could muster. Janis laughed and explained that yes, her husband loved shooting animals, and as a result, she had more trophy heads hanging on walls in her home than she could count and more than she wanted. But the flip side—and something non-hunters don't understand, she told Shannon—is hunters are among the most ardent conservationists in America. They have selfish reasons that can be characterized as "save 'em so you can shoot 'em," but there's more too. Hunters spend a lot of time in the wilderness and the outdoors, and they develop an appreciation for wildlife and the environment. When Janis received an invitation to be on the zoo board, Fowler backed her completely.

The day in Sedona gave Shannon a chance to visit the Fowlers' property in Oak Creek Canyon. She saw the red rock formations that draw people to Sedona, but the Fowlers lived nowhere near them. Instead, their property straddled Oak Creek, which made it lush with vegetation, heavily treed and very private. It seemed like a great refuge from the unrelenting heat of a Phoenix summer, Shannon said. She and Janis spent most of the day just walking around the property, scaring the occasional toad along the creek and enjoying the November breeze.

Shannon said she really felt a bond with Janis, who was, as Shannon's mother had been, the wife of a CEO. Although Shannon never knew her mother, she knew about her through her father's stories and memories.

Brent Harrison met Sally at Fordham University, a Jesuit school. Brent majored in chemistry with a minor in business; Sally majored in art history. They both came from upper middle class families. Unlike my folks, Brent and Sally learned early on how to maneuver through charity balls and which fork to use with which course.

Neither family, though, had amassed the wealth Brent created through Harrison Chemicals, which sold industrial bleach. Shannon called it a simple business. Just mix chlorine and caustic soda, and you have bleach. Safety issues exist, but they can be overcome with good worker training, good processes and a healthy respect for the raw ingredients.

The main market consisted of cities and towns that use bleach for water and wastewater disinfection. Brent had built up an effective Northeast network of manufacturing sites, terminals and trucks. He sold into Boston, New York, Philadelphia and a variety of smaller cities and towns, and his volume reached into the hundreds of millions of gallons. Even at 80 cents a gallon, he made railcars full of money for 30 years. When it came time to retire, he sold the company for $127 million.

After Brent and Sally had been married for seven years, they felt settled enough to consider starting a family. Brent told Shannon her mother had been more excited by the prospect of having her than by anything he could remember.

Once Sally became pregnant, she and Brent decided to be surprised by the sex of the baby, but they chose the name Shannon as one that could work for either a boy or a girl. They liked the meaning—wise river—which derived from a goddess in Irish mythology.

Sally had an uneventful pregnancy, and her doctors didn't know until delivery began about her placenta accreta. The condition occurs when blood vessels and other parts of the placenta grow too deeply into the uterine wall. Immediately after delivery, Sally experienced heavy vaginal bleeding as the placenta tore from the uterus. Doctors tried everything they knew to stop the bleeding, but they failed, and Brent did his best to raise Shannon alone.

He hired a nanny, and he tried to be an attentive father, but he never really found a way to come to terms with the hole left in his heart by Sally's death. Shannon said it felt as though he hesitated to love her fully because he never wanted to feel the immense pain he would know if he lost her. He never faced that problem, though, dying in the plane crash just three years after selling his company. Shannon had just graduated from Fordham, good old "FU," as she calls it, so like me, she had more than a dose of Catholicism in her background. Like her mom, she also majored in art history. Unlike her mom—and unlike me, for that matter— she became a multimillionaire before she turned 23.

Shannon eventually recovered, and she never lost her ability to have a good time. But we both understood she constantly hungered for surrogate parents. She and my mom had a strong bond, and Janis filled the bill as well, much as that made me uncomfortable.

"Janis came from nowhere, really. I mean, Staten Island! But she lucked out by marrying her hard-driving husband,"

Shannon said. "Imagine coming from a blue-collar background to marry a guy who became a multimillionaire! And she's developed herself over the years to become a real asset to him. She's well read, gracious, and she tells me she's become a decent club tennis player over the years. Truth is, she has enough personality and heart for both of them."

While they visited in Sedona, Janis told Shannon she occupied much of her time by administering the Fowler Family Foundation.

"So Fowler has his own foundation?" I asked. "He doesn't strike me as the kind of guy who'd give a rat's ass about charities and donations."

"Yeah, you're mostly right. Janis said Red Metal is a major contributor to the United Way. During the drive each year, Jeff tells employees he gives his fair share and more to the United Way because he can always trust the money is being used well and with a minimum of administrative expense. Janis says that's true, but it's also true that giving to United Way is an obligation of his position. He doesn't want to spend any time learning about what different charities and nonprofits do. A charity is a charity, as far as he's concerned, whether it helps the homeless or mentally handicapped kids, so why not just give money to the United Way and let them hand it out however they will."

Which is why Janis became the driving force behind the Fowler Family Foundation. Many in her circle of friends had a family foundation, so she encountered the twin motivations of peer pressure and keeping up with the Joneses. She also wanted to teach her kids about being involved in community causes. She sold it to Fowler by emphasizing the tax breaks. She kept him happy by supporting programs of conservation groups he cared about, like Ducks Unlimited, the Rocky Mountain Elk Foundation, and, of course, the Phoenix Zoo.

"Janis said she also appealed to the control freak in her husband. She told him if they had their own foundation, they could control who sat on the board, who gets the money, and how the money gets used. He bit, but Janis thinks he probably wanted to keep her happy more than anything else."

Then Shannon made a pitch of her own.

"You know, Dave, the Brown Family Foundation has a nice ring to it. You know, even trinkets and trips get old. I enjoy my junkets with Jessica. I'm not complaining. But maybe it's time for us to start giving something back, to add more substance to our lives."

My first thought, I'll admit, seemed pretty cold. Shannon came into this marriage with millions of her own money. If she wanted to start a foundation, why not just use some of it? She got hers the easy way, by inheriting it. I worked hard for every penny I had, and I wasn't ready just yet to think about giving it away. But I didn't say that.

"If you want, let's study how to go about it, then we can talk about it later." And with that, we both decided we'd join Gary and Jessica in their nap.

• • •

The holidays brought with them all the things Shannon and I love about New York in winter. Playing with the toys at FAO Schwarz, even if we didn't have kids. Watching the skaters while standing next to the towering Christmas tree at Rockefeller Center. And yes, heading to Radio City Music Hall for the Rockettes. We let ourselves be unashamedly corny for this one brief period each year. We even had Santa pajamas for the holidays—still do, in fact. Actually, mine are pajamas, hers is a Mrs. Santa, see-through, red-and-white negligee, which works just fine for me.

Gary and I used the holiday lull to keep increasing our position in Red Metal. Through a combination of stock and options, we controlled about 10 percent of the company by February 2006.

Shannon received a Christmas card from Janis saying she'd love to stay in touch, but Fowler and I had no further communication after our trip to Mordecai. Then in early February, a letter arrived:

Dear Mr. Brown:

We at Red Metal have taken note of the increasing interest of Galileo Capital in our company. We would like to discuss with you the possibility of joining our board.

In our January meeting, I briefed board members on our discussions last November. They decided it could be good to have you on the board to represent your views, which seem to resonate with a small portion of our other shareholders. At the same time, we believe you might benefit by gaining more insight into the many, complicated factors that enter into decisions about how to deploy cash in today's global mining environment.

We are eager to have you join us. The compensation is meager—$150,000 a year plus expenses and other miscellaneous benefits—but I believe you would find the experience to be beneficial on many levels.

I would be happy to discuss board membership at your convenience. Please call me so we can review any questions or concerns you might have.

Sincerely,
Jeff Fowler

He had cc'd all his board members. I told Gary to come to my office immediately.

"Read this," I told him. He concentrated on the letter for a couple of minutes. Then, he laid it down and laughed. Uncontrollably.

Finally, he calmed down and asked, "Can you spell 'co-opt'?"

"There's no way Fowler told the board he enjoyed our time together. Or that he thought I'd be a stellar board member. I imagine spending time with me is his second favorite thing, right behind catching bowling balls with his teeth. So, somebody in the room figured we could be reined in by making me a member of the club."

"They're your kind of folks, for sure. You know ... an oil company CEO, a firearms CEO, a coal-mining CEO. A few retired CEOs, for good measure. A token female/minority academic to check the boxes on those fronts. And several more where they came from."

"Yeah, to make it perfect, they need to throw in a CEO of a private prison company. Can they really believe we'd consider this, even for a minute? Let's send them a signal. Go buy some more Red Metal stock!"

Here's the response I dictated:

Dear Mr. Fowler:

Thank you for your offer to discuss the possibility of joining Red Metal's board of directors. We have decided, however, that Galileo Capital and I can continue to be a more effective advocate for shareholders in our present circumstances.

If I joined your board, I would feel ethically constrained to support its decisions, even if I believed the company could do more for shareholders. I understand in a board setting, opposing views can be aired, but once a decision is made, a good board member rallies behind it whether or not he agrees with it. I doubt I would be able to do so.

I note with disbelief just how little Red Metal stock each of your board members owns. Because of this, I question just how well the board's interests are aligned with shareholders. Rather than join a group outnumbering me 11 to 1, I choose to remain independent and advocate publicly on behalf of shareholders.

I will continue to say Red Metal remains overcapitalized, to speak euphemistically. In plain English, your balance sheet is undermanaged and bloated with far too much cash.

Copper prices have continued to rise dramatically during the time we have been accumulating Red Metal stock. If you fail to manage your cash effectively, either by buying your stock back or making solid acquisitions, you will be acquired yourself. Taking one of these actions is your best assurance to maintain your status as an independent, publicly traded company.

I, in fact, would encourage you to take an even bolder step: Borrow money now to give shareholders a real boost, then pay back the loan. Buy back a significant portion of your stock and pay out a large special dividend. With copper prices where they are, you will be able to pay the loan back in short order. In the meantime, the debt you take on will be further assurance against your being acquired.

If your board is not agreeable to returning more cash to shareholders, we are prepared to work with other shareholders to force you to maximize value for us. We also are prepared to seek out potential acquirers for Red Metal if it proves to be our best course for maximizing value. We are engaging advisors to help us develop our options and will keep you advised of our actions.

Yours truly,
David Brown

I let Gary read the letter.

"So, you're engaging advisors without talking it over with me?"

"Of course not, stupid. We'll start looking around today. Give George Petersen a call over at Ameribank, and check with Sally Smithers at Gloucester. Advisors are a dime a dozen. We'll have a team put together—or at least forming—before Fowler receives the letter. And we'll send it FedEx Priority so he'll have it tomorrow."

As soon as Beth had it ready to go, I gave her one more instruction: Make sure our lawyers get the letter filed with the SEC tomorrow, and get it into the hands of Jim Stevenson at Bloomberg first thing in the morning.

●　　●　　●

By the close of market the next afternoon—two o'clock Phoenix time—Red Metal issued a news release. That signaled quick turnaround for a company like theirs, which usually vets public statements through PR people, IR people, lawyers, accountants and who knows how many outside consultants. Corporate buddies have told me it can take three weeks of review for an important news release. We struck a nerve.

Fowler called our proposal a reckless bet on copper price trends that could threaten Red Metal's future. He said we failed to recognize the complexities of managing a commodity-based business in the face of unpredictable commodity-price swings. He said Red Metal meets regularly with investors—including Galileo—and listens carefully to their views. And, of course, he reiterated the company's four priorities—invest in existing businesses, improve the quality of its asset base, strengthen its balance sheet, and finally, reward shareholders.

"We are absolutely committed to returning substantial cash to our shareholders as our actual results warrant it," he said.

No sooner had I read the release than Beth buzzed me to say Jim Stevenson from Bloomberg wanted to talk.

"So, Jim, have you called Fowler?"

"Yeah, about 15 minutes ago. He used a speakerphone, so you know he had other people in the room with him. I always wonder what kinds of hand signs and shorthand they have to communicate with one another. A couple of times he just put me on mute while they talked among themselves."

"So, what did you learn?"

"They stick to the script as well as anyone. I can tell they've dropped quite a few dollars on media training. They're trained to say up front they have only a few minutes to talk, but I find if they think an interview is going well, they'll talk forever."

"Good, Jim. But what did you learn?"

"Not anything you wouldn't expect. He's really ticked off you went public with your letter. Said it showed a lack of class."

"Well, you know, what choice did we have? It's material to shareholders that we're looking at shopping the company around if Red Metal doesn't step up to treat its investors the way they should be treated. It's not something you can keep to yourself."

"So that's the booster rocket you're going to strap onto Red Metal stock. Find another company to buy it at a premium from an already record-high price."

"It's possible, Jim. But it's not inevitable. Red Metal holds its future in its hands. If it treats shareholders right, it can determine its own destiny."

"And if not?"

"Well, let's give them a chance and see what they do."

I, of course, counted on them to do the wrong thing.

NINE

Gary and I assembled our team of advisors from the likes of Ameribank and Gloucester, two common names in the world of mergers, acquisitions and restructuring schemes. We saw quickly how they made money; they staffed up our account with lots of high-billing consultants. Even their secretarial help billed out at $200 an hour. We pulled the plug after a month.

We already knew what they offered as their major piece of advice: Meet with other major shareholders to gauge their sentiment about Red Metal. What we learned didn't surprise us. The pension funds holding Red Metal stock loved its performance and the special dividend the company had granted. Most of the mutual funds felt the same way. We did, however, confirm one thing: The company's investor relations skills stank.

Wayne Luboff, who ran the Pimlico Growth Fund, said it best. "They're always dumping their IR executives, and I can't figure out why. They've all been responsive to me, and they do a good job of keeping in touch. But then one day, they're gone, and I'm dealing with someone new. All I can figure is it's personal chemistry. They get along fine with me, but my read is they have a tough audience inside the company, and sooner or later, it's time to show one the door and audition the next one.

"On the rare occasions Fowler or the CFO comes to see us, there's no time for chitchat, lunch or dinner. I'm not looking for anything extravagant, but some evidence of the social graces would be appreciated. They present the facts, pretend to answer my questions, and scoot off down the road to their next meeting. Definitely a 'slam, bam, thank you ma'am' encounter every time. We're an obligation to be met, not a partner to be valued. That's how it feels to me. Which is okay, I suppose, as long as they're delivering the goods.

"We've held their stock for years, and except for the time copper tanked so badly a few years ago, it's always been a reliable part of our portfolio. The past couple of years it's been the leader. The good news for them boils down to this: the spotlight has turned their way. The bad news? The spotlight has turned their way. They've moved from supporting cast in many portfolios to the star of the show. We'll see whether they can carry the load from here on out.

"If they make a significant move, I'll hear them out. But I'd be more inclined to give them the benefit of the doubt if they took more time with me once in a while."

I heard the same message several times. The Fowler who pissed me off so adeptly hadn't developed any Dale Carnegie skills with other investors, either. Nobody (except Gary and me) would turn on him as long as the stock price rose and Red Metal threw out a little extra dividend money from time to time; not everyone hungered as much as Gary and I to get our hands on more cash. But then again, no one I met would quickly rally to his side or offer up testimonials about his skill as a strategic leader.

• • •

In graduate school, one of my profs used to say that to a businessman, no scarier words existed than "*60 Minutes* is outside, and they want to talk with you." Gary and I found something scarier.

On the morning of February 21, 2006, two FBI agents stood outside our office doors in the usual attire—black suits, black ties, and matching scowls. If you'd added a couple of black fedoras, they could have been Jake and Elwood Blues. Except Jake and Elwood couldn't threaten to haul us in. Office hours didn't begin until nine o'clock, but we showed up at eight, and it looked as though they'd been waiting for a while.

Gary and I had just finished breakfast at Junior's in Grand Central Station. Cheesecake draws in the crowds, but for breakfast, I went with lox and bagels. Gary played it Midwest-safe with an order of oatmeal with raisins and cinnamon.

Not that FBI agents Katz and Hardaway cared about our breakfast selections, and the sight of them set the lox and bagels battling within my stomach. After identifying themselves, they said they had a few questions and invited themselves inside.

We went into our conference room, and Gary and I sat side by side. Katz and Hardaway sat across from us, making a point of saying our digs must have cost a fortune. If they flipped a coin to see who would play good cop, it must have landed on edge.

We offered them coffee or water. They passed.

"What brings you here today?" I asked. "Oh, I know. You couldn't come yesterday because of the federal holiday, right?" My little joke about President's Day drew not even the hint of a smile.

"Seriously, we've done nothing wrong. We have two compliance officers on staff, which is one more than most firms our size. We'll answer your questions, but what would bring you to our door anyway?"

After making it clear they'd be asking the questions, not us, Katz and Hardaway said the FBI had teamed with the SEC to investigate us. They wanted to know how we became interested in Red Metal stock. Gary, as usual, wanted no part of talking on behalf of Galileo. That job fell to me.

Investors invest, I said. Red Metal had attracted the attention of many Wall Street firms. We studied the company and the dynamics of the copper market, and Red Metal raised up its head and called out for our money.

"Is copper an industry you always follow?" Hardaway asked.

There's no such thing, I explained. We keep an eye on sectors to see which ones are turning cold and which ones are heating up. We can make money either way. When we saw the basic materials sector heat up, we paid attention. We thought Red Metal gave us the best chance to make some real money.

"Maybe so, but not everybody decided to own 5 percent of the company initially and even more since," Katz said.

"Not everybody can!" I snorted. "Our investors put their money with us—lots of it—and they trust us to make more for them than anyone else can. When we decided what we wanted to do, we made it happen."

Hardaway said owning so much of any one company seemed like a big risk.

"No risk, no reward." By now, I really had become pissed off. "Our investors don't expect or want us to be pansies. And besides, as long as we do it legally, what business is it of the SEC or the FBI how we use our money, and whether we make a pile or lose a pile?"

"Look," Hardaway said. "The SEC is hearing you might have acted on insider information to move on Red Metal.

They've asked us to take a look at your books, your logs, your phone records. Give us access to those, and we might be able to clear this up quickly."

"Hell, no! Bring a warrant, and we'll talk. And next time you come, phone ahead. I'd like to have a lawyer with us if you come back. Which I doubt you'll do, 'cause there's nothing to this. We didn't know a soul within Red Metal before we started buying the stock. We didn't know any insiders. And we haven't exactly made ourselves popular with them. Who's saying we had insider information, anyway?"

He didn't answer.

"And who exactly gave the order for you two to visit us today? Who's your boss? Who can we talk to at the FBI?"

Clearly, Katz and Hardaway didn't want to finger their boss. Hardaway offered up another name.

"The SEC enforcement office here is headed by Dennis Clobes. Usually when our bosses send us out on a case like this, he makes the request."

Katz and Hardaway left. By then, our small band of employees had arrived, and several gawked at the agents as they walked out. Their off-the-rack suits might not exactly have pegged them as FBI, but they didn't have the well-heeled look of our typical clients.

Gary and I spent some time in silence in the conference room. Trouble has a way of putting a damper on conversation. Finally, I forced some words out of my mouth.

"We're not guilty, but guilty or not, if people hear the FBI and the SEC are poking around our offices, investors will get nervous. And nervous investors pull their money and go elsewhere as soon as they can. I can't see any possibly good ending to this little encounter the government is having with us."

No reason to panic, Gary told me, walking me off the ledge, as he had so many times before. His suggestion: Let's learn more about this Dennis Clobes and what might motivate him to want to give us grief. He said he'd take on that job.

TEN

The FBI visit rattled me, but life has to go on, right? And so, as Gary began looking into Clobes, I got back to work on making things happen for us at Red Metal.

I needed to make good on my threat to seek out acquirers for the company. More important, I needed Red Metal to hear I was actively seeking buyers.

Galileo had brokered the sale of Mangelsdorf Pharmaceuticals, so no one doubted our ability to make deals happen. But if Fowler felt complacent, nothing would give him the willies more than hearing about us shopping the company around. As he'd showed me in November, he greatly feared having the Red Metal name fade into oblivion on his watch. I could rattle him in a hurry by ginning up rumors we had a buyer on the line.

Common wisdom would be that a bigger fish was needed to gobble up Red Metal. If that had been true, I would have had to book a flight to England or Australia to find someone with the wherewithal to make a run at the company. Instead, in April, I traveled to Birmingham, Alabama.

I'd noticed with every earnings release, Don Cunningham, the CEO of Fletcher-Broussard Copper Company, stopped by to have his quarterly chat with one of the CNBC infobabes. In fact, he seemed to be available to anyone who wanted to talk, and the programs usually had a hard time shutting him down to cut to commercial. I wouldn't necessarily call him a ham, but he would have been right at home next to a plate of green eggs.

People who'd met him, though, gladly looked beyond his showboating. He had a way of making people feel appreciated, and shareholders in Fletcher-Broussard thought the world of him. And apparently, his gift of gab made him a good interview.

Jim Ewald, a buddy of mine who started Ewald Capital down the street from our offices, told me he really liked the guy. "He makes it a point to at least call whenever he's in town, and he's more than happy to take me and my wife out to dinner. He's smart—graduated at the top of his class at Kentucky—but he's as approachable as your favorite uncle. You wouldn't know to visit with him that he and Jerry Jack Miller have convinced their board to pay each of them $35 million or so a year. I'm not saying they're not worth it—hell, if you can get somebody to pay you that kind of money for running a small copper company, you're worth it, at least to somebody—but I'd have to say it's excessive compared to other companies in their space.

"I don't really care, though. I get a kick out of the guy, and Jerry Jack's even more of a hoot. Does the best impression of Jerry Lee Lewis you'd ever want to see. They make money, they treat their shareholders well, and that's really what it's all about, right? So I'm not going to begrudge them their take-home pay."

Jim hit on the reason most people wouldn't think about Fletcher-Broussard as a company to acquire Red Metal. With a market cap of about $10 billion, Fletcher-Broussard weighed in at half the size of Red Metal. But that didn't stop Don and Jerry Jack, the chairman, from spending time with me in Birmingham.

The Fletcher-Broussard offices took up four of the top floors of the AmSouth Center in downtown Birmingham. The building, completed in 1972, stands 30 floors tall. Like many buildings from that era, it features a reflective glass skin on all four sides. It oozed modern in the early '70s.

The FB offices themselves stood in stark contrast. I stepped off the elevator and into a foyer that could have been lifted from an antebellum plantation mansion—floor-to-ceiling, dark mahogany paneling; a plush, beige, cut-pile carpet; dark-brown leather chairs; a mahogany coffee table; built-in mahogany bookshelves stocked with exquisite mineral samples and plenty of pictures of Don and Jerry Jack with presidents and kings; and a receptionist named Sherri Dodson, a brunette who had chosen a form-fitting, black-and-white, polka-dot dress for her work day. The company had the offices behind Sherri locked down tight. You didn't get in unless Sherri buzzed you in.

"Sherri, I swear you just walked out of the pages of Cosmopolitan. My name's David Brown, and I'm here to visit with Don Cunningham and Jerry Jack Miller."

She flashed a Southern belle smile and said she'd been expecting me.

"I'll let them know you're here. While you're waiting, could I get you some coffee or sweet tea? You're from New York, right? You can't come to the South and not drink a little sweet tea."

I asked for a glass of water. I had sweet tea once in Memphis. If you let it evaporate from the glass, you'd be left with a big chunk of tea-colored rock candy. I imagined my insides would be coated with sugar if I indulged in sweet tea.

Eventually, Jerry Jack's assistant, Peggy, came to lead me through the fortress doors.

"Jerry Jack and Don want to have lunch with you in our executive dining room," she said. "I hope you haven't eaten."

"No. I'm starving!"

I had grabbed a quick burger at the airport, but I psyched myself up to take on a few extra calories in the name of business. It would have been impolite to refuse a meal. No sense violating the social graces on a visit to Dixie.

Peggy led me into the dining room, which could seat about 50. The interior decorator mimicked the look of the foyer—more mahogany, but used as wainscoting; a light, elegantly patterned wallpaper; crown molding; more of the carpet used in the foyer; and a large bar as well stocked as Sir Harry's at the Waldorf. Windowless walls surrounded us. Five African-American waiters moved among the tables. They wore white Eton jackets and white gloves, and they stood along a side wall with white towels draped over their forearms as they waited to serve.

Jerry Jack and Don stood as we approached their table and greeted me like an old college chum. Don looked to be in his late 50s and well-traveled, not in a good way. He hunched over a bit, wearing a white dress shirt and a blue tie that followed the contours of an ample waistline. His hair had turned white with grayish highlights. His smile exaggerated the bags beneath his eyes, gray and reddened but ever alert. I had no doubt that behind them sat the active, calculating mind of a dealmaker.

Jerry Jack stood half a head taller than Don, and he appeared to be at least a decade older. Even so, he carried himself like a trim, disciplined soldier. His hair had been dyed jet black one too many times; it might have started out shiny and bright, but somewhere it had taken on more of a matte finish. I read he had fought off some serious diseases in his day—everything from malaria to cancer. He amazed me by looking as good as he did. I knew both of these men had led a harder life than mine; they were hands-on executives, and that's the toll taken by traipsing around the world in search of mineral wealth.

When we sat down, Jerry Jack explained he'd built the dining room because no restaurant in Birmingham lived up to his standards. Besides, he felt safer staying in the building than venturing out where someone might try to harass him and Don or, God knows, kidnap one of them for ransom money. It sounded paranoid to me, but they spent lots of time in third-world countries and I didn't, so maybe they had it right.

Little time elapsed before a waiter came to our table.

"Welcome to our dining room, Mr. David. Mr. Donald and Mr. Jerry Jack told me you'd be joining us. My name's James. What can I get you to drink?"

Both Jerry Jack and Don sat well supplied with hard liquor.

"James, how are you set for single-malt scotch?"

"We have a Glenlivet 12-year-old or a Glenfiddich 12-year-old."

I ordered a Glenlivet and then took a minute to study the menu of the day, settling on the Kobe beef steak. Not bad for a company-run dining room.

Don and Jerry Jack had been part of a mutual admiration society for about 30 years. Jerry Jack made his millions in oil. When they met, Don enjoyed a reputation as an up-and-coming accountant at one of the Big Eight firms, and Don gave Jerry Jack an education in how to hold onto more of his millions. Jerry Jack hired Don for twice his Big Eight salary, and within a couple of years, Don found himself as the CFO for Fletcher-Broussard. Lots of what was then privately held stock and hefty dividends had made Don a rich man, and he jumped from rich to wealthy when the company went public. They lived in Birmingham because Jerry Jack grew up there, and he couldn't imagine living any other place.

"Don and I met when I still saw the oil business as my true love," Jerry Jack said. "One day, one of our geologists headed to Peru to explore for oil. He came up dry but stumbled upon one of the largest copper deposits in the world. Oil had fallen into the shitter anyway, so I said to Don, I said, 'What do you think about chucking oil and going into copper?' We did a couple of days of research and not too long after, made the pivot into copper.

"Within a few years, we took the company public. Needless to say, we've done okay for ourselves. We only own one mine, but it's a doozy. Most years we take more copper and molybdenum out of the ground than any other single mine in the world. I'm sure you know we got even luckier when we struck gold in the same deposit."

I did. Copper and molybdenum paid out handsomely at the moment, but in the down times, gold had always helped level out the roller-coaster ride of the copper price cycle for Fletcher-Broussard.

Don asked me to tell him about myself, specifically how I became interested in finance as a career. My dad's life as a meat cutter had no appeal for me. I loved math and numbers in high school. During a career day at Fenwick, an executive from Goldman Sachs told us about the calculations he did to determine which of several investments offered to his company had the best chance of returning the most money in the shortest time. He also told us how quickly he made his first million. He couldn't have been more than 15 years older than us.

"I knew then and there I wanted to be part of his world. The priests at Fenwick told us about the freedom of a life of service. I figured I could learn more about that, if I wanted, after I found the freedom of indulging whatever whim I had. A career in finance appeared to be my quickest path to that goal, and when Wharton accepted me, the deal was sealed."

"Sounds like we all grew up hungry," Don said. "My dad worked all his life as a gas-station attendant. Jerry Jack's dad died when Jerry Jack turned eight, so he learned to fend for himself pretty early in life. We both grew up Southern Baptist, but, well, we've never let it interfere with the enjoyment of the finer things in life, or even some of the questionable ones!

"So, David, are you here for real to talk with us about buying Red Metal, or are you just trying to yank Jeff Fowler's chain? Not that it matters too much to us. We get a kick out of yanking Jeff's chain whenever the opportunity presents itself."

It turned out Fowler, Cunningham and Miller had met on more than one occasion. They all enjoyed hunting, and they had gotten together several times to hunt in Chile before CESCO, the big world copper conference each spring in Santiago.

"The way things played out, we hunted together three times, and our luck rotated. First year, Jerry Jack brings down a red stag, and Jeff and I bag nothing. Second year, I shoot a stag, and Jerry Jack and Jeff come up empty handed. Third year, Jeff takes down a stag—the biggest of all three—and Jerry Jack and I strike out. We all donated the meat to a local charity that feeds poor people.

"When we arrived at CESCO, the three of us attended a private cocktail reception, and to give him the benefit of the doubt, let's just say Jeff appeared to have had one too many

Manhattans. Oh, they make a good Manhattan in Santiago! He told anyone he could find about how his stag dwarfed the ones we had taken down. Like anyone cared. And he kept saying something about how the size of the stag must be determined by the size of the operations we ran. To anyone who would listen.

"No one could shut him up until somebody rolled out a piano and asked Jerry Jack to do his Jerry Lee Lewis impression. Jeff lost his audience, and he left in a huff after *Great Balls of Fire*. We haven't spoken a dozen words since."

"Well, to answer your question, I'm serious about you two taking a run at Red Metal. Would you entertain the idea? The thing I like about you both is you don't run from opportunity when you see it. And this could be a big opportunity for Fletcher-Broussard."

"I see how it could be a big opportunity for you, us gobbling up all your stock for zillions more than you paid for it," Jerry Jack said. "But I'm not so sure it's a great opportunity for us. Those Red Metal mines aren't nearly as high a quality as our mine in Peru. They're making great money now, of course, but their ore is nothing like ours. I'm not thrilled about digging up 1,000 pounds of rock to come away with two pounds of copper."

"Well, four pounds, actually, and that's not unusual, as you know better than I do. Those older mines still have lots of life left in them. And you can't overlook some of the projects they're working on. They own a property in Africa with an ore grade 10 times better than anything they're working today."

"Yeah, good luck getting that one up and running. I've read about it. Out in the middle of nowhere with shitty roads to the nearest major town 300 miles away. And with a bunch of natives scarfing up a little ore here and there to sell to who knows who, all to scrape some money together for food. You're not going to be able to run a mine that makes any sense in a situation like that."

As Jerry Jack and I bantered back and forth, Don had asked James to bring him a calculator, some paper and a pencil. He laid down some numbers, and then more numbers. Whatever he was doing, it appeared to be as neat and organized as any spreadsheet I'd seen. Eventually he looked up.

"Jerry Jack, take a look at this. I know we'd be taking on a lot, but I took a shot at where Red Metal can be—short-term and long-term—if copper hits a certain price and stays anywhere within a not-too-tight range for a few years. We just might have to take David's proposition seriously at some point."

Jerry Jack studied Don's calculations for a couple of minutes. I just watched as his brow furrowed, he scratched his head, he did his own mental calculations, and he asked Don for the pencil to scribble a few more items on the paper. Finally, he turned to Don.

"I guess it's possible this could work for us and make our friend here a lot of money. It all hinges on copper hitting somewhere close to what you wrote down here."

"Do you mind my asking what that figure would be?"

Jerry Jack smiled and then folded the paper into thirds and tucked it into his coat pocket.

"David, I'd have to call that proprietary at the moment. I can tell you we're not there yet, and of course, it's impossible to know whether we'll ever be there. I don't want to get your hopes up, but it's not impossible we could be interested in taking a run at Jeff someday, if we can make the numbers work. Who knows? Don and I might yet come away with the biggest stag."

With that, Jerry Jack asked James to bring us all some coffee and pecan pie. I'm a Northerner through and through, but I could see Southern living had its advantages, especially if you could live like Don and Jerry Jack.

We said our goodbyes, promising to keep in touch, and I headed for the Birmingham-Shuttlesworth International Airport. (I get a kick out of these small town "international" airports. Bring in a few flights from Mexico, Canada or the Caribbean, and suddenly you're "international.") Before I departed, I made a call to Todd Williamson, Red Metal's IR guy. Like me or not, as Red Metal's biggest shareholder, he had to talk with me.

I asked a few questions about copper prices and how Red Metal's efforts to control its costs were coming along. Mainly, though, I wanted to mention I was calling from the Birmingham airport.

"Really?" he said. "What took you to Birmingham?" As if he couldn't figure it out.

I said I grew up in Chicago and always admired Michael Jordan. I had a little time on my hands, and I wanted to see Regions Park, where Jordan spent his one season in minor league baseball with the Birmingham Barons.

"Yeah, right. I'm guessing you probably had occasion to meet a young woman named—oh, what's her name?— Sherri while you've been there. If you've met her, you know who I mean."

I had to smile. Apparently, Todd had a libido and a life outside copper and stock prices, and he had a bit of subtlety and wit about him. Good to know Red Metal had at least one human on board with a pulse.

"Yeah, I think I did run into a Sherri. Downtown, the AmSouth Building. Yeah. She sends you her regards, or I think she would have if I'd mentioned your name. Thanks for the conversation."

I hung up, confident that Fowler would know within minutes I'd had a visit with my new friends, Jerry Jack and Don.

ELEVEN

Back in New York, Gary had briefed our employees on our visit from the FBI. We had no reason to panic, he told them, as he had told me. He also instructed them to be careful both inside the office and out. We had done nothing wrong, but we needed to control the flow of information, and we needed to know exactly what the government sought.

"We had a staff meeting," Gary told me when I returned from Birmingham. "I told everyone to inform us if anyone from the SEC or FBI tries to contact them. I said to refer them to us, and always let us know exactly what kind of information they're trying to get."

So we had the staff locked down pretty well, as long as no one got spooked. We didn't want some innocuous but poorly stated comment by one of our folks to open up an even bigger mess.

Within a couple of days of my return from Birmingham, one of our employees, Andy Ruby, asked for a meeting with Gary and me.

"At the Starbucks downstairs just now, when my turn came to order, this dark-suited guy with slicked-back hair steps next to me and tells the counter girl he'd be paying for my drink. He then orders for me—a nonfat, no-whip grande mocha. Which is what I always get, so he must have been watching me for a while.

"He hands me the drink and leads me to a table. Tells me he's Jim Katz from the FBI and he'd spent some time with both of you lately. I told him I'd heard, but I really didn't know any specifics. He said he'd also heard I might know about the company's inner sanctum because Galileo saw me as an up-and-comer. Which I took as so much bullshit. Then he starts asking whether I'm happy at Galileo and whether I think it's well run. By which he meant, he said, on the up and up.

"I told him I think the world of Galileo and you two and I had no interest in continuing the conversation. I left the drink on the table. Never even had a sip. He tried to get me to stay, but I figured if I kept on walking and he didn't stop me, then he really didn't have any power to make me talk to him. So I left, but I wanted you both to know right away. The really scary thing for me, though, is as I started to walk out the door, he yelled, 'Say hello to Sally, Sam and Jack for me.' Why does he know the names of my wife and kids? I don't know why he's trying to suck me and my family into this, but I don't like it."

Gary and I thanked Andy for letting us know, and we assured him we'd do everything we could to keep Katz or any other agent from bothering him again. We said we'd always run Galileo to comply with both the spirit and the letter of the law, so we didn't worry about that, and he shouldn't either.

I told Gary to come with me to my office, and we called Katz. I knew Gary wouldn't say anything, but I wanted him to hear the conversation.

"Katz, what's the big idea, shaking up Andy Ruby? He has nothing to do with this, and certainly nothing to offer you and your 'investigation.' Stay away from our employees."

"I'm an agent of the FBI. I'll talk to whoever the hell I please, whenever the hell I please, wherever the hell I please."

"A conversation is one thing, but since when did the FBI start using mob tactics? Stalking him, ordering the drink he drinks, letting him know you know the names of his wife and kids. If you think you have something on us, lay it out on the table, but leave our employees out of it. No more of this bullshit intimidation!" I slammed down the phone.

Once I cooled down, I asked Gary whether he'd made any progress on getting the lowdown on Dennis Clobes at the SEC. He'd put a corporate intel company on the case to keep us low profile. We could expect a report within a week.

• • •

Two days later, Katz and Hardaway walked into our offices, this time with a search warrant and a small herd of accountants and computer nerds.

"FBI! Stop everything you're doing!" Hardaway barked out to our employees. "Hands off the keyboards! Hang up your phones! Don't touch your Blackberries! Do nothing more until we say you can!"

Gary and I heard the ruckus. We darted from our offices. I asked Gary to get our lawyer over to the office immediately. I told our employees to comply, and I ordered the gang of marauders to get into our conference room. No one moved until Katz nodded toward the door.

"Okay, G-men, let's see your warrant. Exactly what are you looking for?"

In fact, Katz and Hardaway had two warrants, one to search our physical records and one to examine computer files for specific information about our dealings in Red Metal stock.

"I don't care what your warrant says. Nobody in this room touches anything until our lawyer arrives."

Gary and I knew Peter Barrows from Fenwick High. He earned his law degree from Yale and then joined Duvalier-Reed, one of New York's many silk-stocking law firms. It took him eight years to become a partner. He's been our lawyer ever since we founded Galileo.

Once he arrived, he perused the warrant.

"So, what's your probable cause? What makes you think there could be evidence of a crime here?"

"That's above my pay grade," Katz said. "We have a warrant, so the judge believes there's probable cause. You can take it up with him. Any other questions?"

Peter told us we had to let them proceed. I told the employees to cooperate but said Peter would be staying with us in case they had specific questions about whether to open a specific record or file. For the next four hours, Gary, Peter and I huddled together in my office while the marauders did their work. They seemed to know how to do their job well. No one came to us to protest anything being asked for. Eventually, Katz, Hardaway and company left with a large stack of paper files, emails and several thumb drives.

"So, what do you think is really going on here?" I asked Peter.

"My guess is somebody's trying to shake you up and maybe shake you down. It wouldn't take much for investors to be spooked by a government investigation, whether it turned out to be warranted or not."

The next morning, The Wall Street Journal reported we had been searched in connection with our Red Metal activities. The calls started coming in immediately, 20 in all.

Our investors are a sophisticated lot. The SEC requires them to be accredited investors, which means they have to have a net worth of at least $1 million, or earned $200,000 in the past two consecutive years (or $300,000 when combined with a spouse) and have a reasonable expectation of making as much in the future. We set tougher requirements; investors had to have at least $5 million in investable assets. All of which is to say our investors usually knew something about money and the ways of the world. Which is not to say they took the news well.

"When it comes to my money, it's real simple," one of them told me. "If you see smoke, run like hell."

"Here's the deal. We've done nothing wrong. This investigation is going nowhere. I'm not sure who struck the match, or why, but this will turn out to be nothing. And when it does, believe me, I will retaliate, or at least make sure our good name is restored."

And when it was, he said, he'd be back. Meantime, he wanted to pull his $20 million. By the end of the day, we had to write checks for about $200 million total.

Most of the investors who left had been with us about four to six years. Our longest-standing clients gave us the benefit of the doubt. The story scared our newest clients, but they couldn't go anywhere because of their two-year lock-up period, a standard feature of our agreements. It helps us avoid liquidity problems while we are in sometimes illiquid investments.

Gary and I knew we had to get this behind us as fast as we could. We'd seen more than one hedge fund fold because of scandal, deserved or not.

TWELVE

Aweek later, our corporate intel guy, Ben Becker, invited us to lunch at P.J. Clarke's, where Johnny Mercer wrote the lyrics to *One for My Baby* on a napkin. If you go, don't be rattled by the human leg bones above the entrance. They're an Irish good-luck charm.

After we placed our orders—I went with the King George's Shepherd's Pie—Ben downloaded what he had learned about Dennis Clobes.

"There's nothing really stellar here," Ben said. "Clobes is 55. He lives in Brooklyn Heights and takes the subway to work. Gets off at the Chambers Street Station and walks to his office at 200 Vesey Street.

"He's maybe a little sharper than a marble. Not much. He comes from a little town in Missouri called Mexico, which is best known as the home of Senator Kit Bond. Clobes's dad worked in Mexico as a laborer for A.P. Green Industries, which Bond's grandfather founded. The company makes fire bricks. Decidedly low tech.

"Clobes joined the SEC 25 years ago after scraping through law school at the University of Missouri. Private practice probably wouldn't come looking for him unless he wanted to be a small-town lawyer in Mexico, Hannibal or some other back-water Missouri town. I imagine he saw the SEC as steady, secure and reasonably lucrative for a guy of his limited talents. The commission isn't exactly known for the strength of its starting lineup or bench, as you know.

"Clobes started in Washington, did stints in Chicago and Denver, and finally ended up in New York about a decade ago. He might not be much of a lawyer, but he learned agency politics really well, and he landed a plum assignment.

"His high-school grades were nothing to brag about, but he gained a reputation around Missouri as a top football player. Several universities wanted him on their offensive line. And here's the part that will interest you. When it came time to sign, he opted for the warmth of the Southwest and became an Arizona Wildcat."

"So you're telling us he played football with Jeff Fowler?"

"More than played football. He and Fowler roomed together, caroused together and did spring break together a couple of years in Fort Lauderdale. They served as best men at each other's weddings. They still have dinner together whenever Fowler comes to New York."

"Talk about friends in high places! But would Fowler really be dumb enough to ask Clobes to do a number on us? I can't wait to ask him."

Gary and Ben both thought I shouldn't be hasty in acting on our new insights into the relationship between Fowler and Clobes. It would be good ammunition if needed, but we had no reason to use it right now. Gary and Ben had to rein me in from my obsessive need to stomp on Fowler, or Clobes, or both.

We finished lunch, and some faux Irish lass brought us the check.

"This one's on me," Ben said. "And David, remember, the whole value of corporate intel comes with timing. Pull the trigger too soon, and a direct hit might turn into a glancing blow. Shoot too late, and it can look like sour grapes. Shoot when the moment's right, and you can stop an opponent in his tracks. And the world never has to know. One thing to think about, though. When the time comes, should you confront Fowler or Clobes? Let's figure that out later."

•   •   •

During the spring of 2006, the market ran more or less on cruise control. The Dow opened around 10,700 in January and reached 11,300 in April, a climb of about 5½ percent. Certainly nothing for the average investor to sneeze at, but not good enough for us. Our portfolio easily lapped most returns, paced first and foremost by Red Metal.

In a year's time, we'd seen our investment in the company go from about $39 a share to as much as $84. Copper moved from $1.50 to $3.70 a pound. In a word, Dr. Copper had gone on a tear. We combed all the data in all the market sectors, and Gary and I concluded, SEC investigation notwithstanding, we could serve our clients best by keeping tons of our money in Red Metal and pushing Fowler and company to increase buybacks and special dividends.

Then in late June, before the market opened, Shannon and I geared up for a bedroom romp. Things were just getting hot when the phone rang. Gary's name came up on caller ID, so I picked up.

"Turn on CNBC. Do it now."

I reached for the remote, and Shannon shot me her best pissed-off look.

"I wouldn't do this if Gary didn't sound so urgent."

"All right, let's see what's up, but then, let's start back where we left off."

She rested her head on my chest, and we turned on CNBC.

There, live from Toronto, Fowler stood before a banner with these words: Red Metal NICAN. Two men flanked him. I didn't recognize them. What the hell has he done now, I thought.

Todd Williamson stood before a lectern to introduce Fowler, who looked as though he hadn't slept in three days.

"Today will go down as a red-letter day in the mining industry," Fowler said, "and I'm pleased to be joined this morning by Steve Berkman and Ralph Gershon to tell you about the groundbreaking transaction we are pursuing."

Berkman, it turned out, served as chairman and CEO of NICAN, one of the world's largest nickel-mining companies and a revered Canadian institution. Gershon headed Eagle Crest Copper, a smaller Canadian mining company. For about six months, Eagle Crest had been working with NICAN to be taken over on friendly terms. Several other mining firms also wanted to bag Eagle Crest.

Fowler explained Red Metal, NICAN and Eagle Crest would combine through a $40-billion transaction that would create a powerhouse North American mining company. All in, the new company would have an "enterprise value" of $61 billion (based on the stock prices of the three companies, the debt they carried, preferred stock value and investments in various affiliates). The deal would produce a "net benefit" to Canada. (Remember those words. Lawyers added them, I'm sure, for reasons I'll explain later.)

The company and its copper division would be headquartered in Phoenix, but the nickel division would have offices in Toronto, and the new Red Metal NICAN would to be traded on both the New York and the Toronto stock exchanges. Which sounded like a bone—a small bone—thrown to the Canadians. It wouldn't be long before they'd spit it back in Fowler's face.

The deal sounded as though Rube Goldberg had risen from the grave and gone into the finance business. And he came back as Rube the Zombie, not Rube the Christ. Rube would have explained it like this [2]:

Red Metal (**A**) flies to Canada and offers to buy all the outstanding shares of NICAN (**B**) for the equivalent of $72.11. (**C**) This figure would be based on the closing price of Red Metal stock (**D**) and the closing US/Canadian dollar exchange rate (**E**) on Friday, June 23, 2006. Each NICAN shareholder would receive 0.672 shares of Red Metal stock (**F**) and $15.75 per share in cash (**G**). This represents a premium of 23 percent to NICAN's market price as of the close of trading on June 23 (**H**) and a premium of 19 percent (**I**) to the value of the existing, unsolicited offer (**J**) for NICAN by Canadian mining company Hecht Komando.[3]

Simultaneously, NICAN has entered into an agreement with Eagle Crest (**K**) to increase its previous offer (**L**) for Eagle Crest. The new offer (**M**) increases the cash component from $11.25 to $15.75 and the exchange ratio (**N**) from 0.524 shares of NICAN for each share of Eagle Crest to 0.55676

---

[2] I've put all the dollar amounts in approximate U.S. dollars just to keep everything consistent. At the time, a U.S. dollar was about 90 percent of a Canadian dollar.

[3] Yeah, it's true. NICAN was already being pursued, so Red Metal was igniting a battle royale.

shares of NICAN for each share of Eagle Crest. Based upon the value of the consideration (**F, G**) offered by Red Metal for NICAN of $72.11 per share, the implied value (**O**) of the revised offer for Eagle Crest is $55.89 per share, representing a 12 percent premium to Eagle Crest's closing price (**O**) on June 23 and a 19 percent premium to the existing, unsolicited offer (**P**) for Eagle Crest by Extracta plc.[4]

At Red Metal's closing price of $82.95 on June 23 (**Q**), the total to be paid by Red Metal for NICAN and Eagle Crest (**R**) would be about $40 billion.

That's how Rube would have explained it, and that's exactly how Fowler explained it. To all appearances, he did it without cue cards. He then added a few more details:

- The Red Metal-NICAN portion of the transaction would be pursued regardless of whether NICAN succeeded in buying Eagle Crest.

- After the deal closed, Red Metal planned to begin a buyback program of its stock of up to $5 billion.

- Under certain conditions, NICAN would pay Red Metal a breakup fee of $475 million on a standalone basis if the Red Metal-NICAN deal failed to close, or $925 million if its deal with Eagle Crest went through and the Red Metal-NICAN deal failed to close. Under other conditions, Red Metal would pay NICAN a breakup fee of $500 million if the deal failed to close.

---

[4] Oh, yeah, that's right. Red Metal wasn't igniting a battle royale. It was just jumping into the ring. And Extracta already owned 20 percent of Eagle Crest.

- The companies believed they could find $900 million in "synergies" (roughly translated as savings) within two years of coming together. (How many times had I seen these estimates fall through?)

- Red Metal NICAN would operate in 35 countries and employ 35,000 people.

- The usual silk-stocking law firms and money guys—Ameribank, Gloucester, etc.—all had their oars in the water. (And finding all sorts of ways to fill their buckets with cash, I figured, whether the deal closed or not.)

- All the CEOs of all the companies would still have a job after the deal closed, and they'd all get to live in their cities of choice. In addition, the majordomos of Red Metal would still be drawing a paycheck.

- The Red Metal board would expand from 11 to 15 directors, and four would come from NICAN and Eagle Crest.

- The metals product lines from the new company would be copper (4.1 billion pounds, or about $13.4 billion based on 2005 prices); nickel (738 million pounds or $5.8 billion); cobalt (14 million pounds or $210 million); and molybdenum (68 million pounds or $1.9 billion).

When Fowler finished, Berkman and then Gershon took the microphone to say how much they loved the new deal. Then CNBC cut away to the studio anchors, who, like Bloomberg reporters, really didn't handle numbers very well. They blathered on innocuously for a while. I ran some preliminary calculations in my head, then turned off the TV.

"What a mess!" I told Shannon. "It's like he set his own trap, bagged himself and delivered his carcass right to our door."

"Tell me more, but later."

She pulled down my boxers. Gary's name came up again on the caller ID. Shannon glared at me. I let him ring through to voicemail.

THIRTEEN

By the time I showed up at the Galileo offices, Gary had done some research and put together a detailed spreadsheet to figure out the things left unsaid in Red Metal's morning announcement.

"To make this thing work, Red Metal is going to have to borrow $27 billion, and it's going to have to get every last dollar of the $900 million in savings it claims it can produce," he told me. "And here's the deal: Most of that $900 million—about $550 million—comes from bringing NICAN and Eagle Crest together.

"For example, up in the Sudbury Basin in Canada, both companies are pretty much mining the same ore body. Every day, NICAN trucks drive ore around a lightly used mill owned by Eagle Crest and load it into rail cars. The cars then head 30 miles south to another mill that does exactly the same thing as the one right next door. There's millions in savings right there if NICAN just used the Eagle Crest mill. What does Red Metal have up there? Nada. Zilch.

"So, if NICAN can't sew up Eagle Crest, the economics don't have a snowball's chance in hell of working. And if they borrow that much, their balance sheet is going to be a disaster, and who knows whether nickel has the same chance of performing as well as copper over the next few years? Maybe they can pay down the debt pretty quickly, maybe not.

Compared with what they're doing, any ideas we've floated look downright conservative! It's like Fowler decided to jump off a cliff with an umbrella for a parachute."

Within three days, Red Metal's stock price had fallen from nearly $83 to about $76, but that in itself indicated little. It's common for an acquiring company's stock price to fall as the market factors in things like the debt it will be taking on.

Within a week, I received a call from Todd Williamson, Red Metal's VP of investor relations. The company was holding a private luncheon at the Waldorf for major investors, and they had us on the invitation list.

"We want to make sure significant investors like Galileo have all the information you need to feel comfortable with what we're doing. Jeff Fowler will present, and we'll have all our senior management on hand to answer questions. You're welcome to bring a guest. Just let me know whether the time will work for you."

"Todd, I'll tell you right now we'll be there. Me and my partner, Gary Gutzler. Hell, if I had booked reservations to the Riviera, I'd cancel the trip. I can't wait to hear what you guys have to say!"

Todd said the company believed a lot of misperceptions and misinformation about the deal had been flying around since it became public. People needed to learn the upsides of the deal. After the luncheon, he believed, investors would come away with a favorable impression of the acquisition.

It took some persuading to get Gary to agree to go. I assured him he didn't have to say a word. In fact, he'd be put to best use by keeping quiet, watching everything going on and providing his sense of the sentiment of the room so we could compare notes.

And what a show he saw!

Red Metal reserved the private dining salon of the Waldorf's Bull and Bear Prime Steakhouse for the luncheon. The room seats 35 at most, so the investors in attendance had to be the top holders of the stock. The glass French doors let us see New York's elite mingle in one of the city's most historic bars but kept out the lunchtime chatter.

Gary and I scheduled things so we could avoid the cocktail time ahead of lunch, but even so, people hadn't taken their seats when we arrived. Fowler had dressed in full combat mode—wool, navy-blue suit; starched white shirt; red, patterned tie with a complementary red pocket square. "Mingling" would be too strong a word to describe his actions, but he at least stood with a small group and didn't have his nose in a stack of notes. He stayed mum from what I could tell, enduring more than enjoying the polite chitchat that proceeds these affairs. He spotted me when I came in, acknowledging me with a quick nod. I walked over to say hello.

"David, you said you wanted something big. This should qualify."

"It's big," I said. "The question is, is it smart?" He scowled for an instant but regained his composure.

"I'm sure you have your opinions. Let's see what the room has to say. It's time for lunch, so have a seat."

The food went down easily, starting with the Bull and Bear Wedge, proceeding to a choice of beef, salmon or chicken, and ending with New York Cheesecake. The deal wasn't nearly as easy to swallow, and it turned out Gary and I had more allies than we knew.

We sat with the teams from Levitt Brothers and Newberg Partners. The first course gave everyone a chance to loosen up with some wine and make polite conversation. How many kids do you have, did you grow up in New York, where do you live now, what do you do for fun? The usual chitchat.

The main course came, and not surprisingly, we all had ordered some cut of beef. The conversation became meatier, too.

"David, you're making quite a minefield for the boys at Red Metal," said Nat Jenkins from Levitt Brothers. Nat and I had never met, but talk around town had him as a cautious, conservative, old-school investment manager. I knew from public filings Levitt Brothers had owned Red Metal on and off for at least a decade and currently owned about 2 percent of the company. I guessed he came down on the side of Red Metal.

"Honestly, Nat, I feel like there's not much I have to do. They seem perfectly capable of planting their own mines—no pun intended—and then stepping on them."

As the conversation unfolded, Nat never let on where he stood on the deal. He kept asking questions about how Galileo came to be interested in Red Metal and whether we really planned to recruit a buyer if Fowler and his board couldn't satisfy our demands.

"All I can tell you, Nat, is we've done it before with Mangelsdorf. It might be tough for someone to take a run at Red Metal if this deal goes through, but that's a big if. Let's see what happens."

About then, dessert came out, and Todd Williamson stood up to introduce Fowler. Todd made it clear that Red Metal executives had a full schedule in New York and Boston. To make all their appointments, the luncheon would have to end in 45 minutes.

In the 10 days or so since the deal became public, Fowler and Red Metal had done nothing to make it appear less complicated or unwieldy. They'd had time to hone their messages and presentation to get to the deal's most salient points. Instead of allaying fear and distrust, however, Fowler seemed to fan the flames of outrage with each slide that materialized on the screen.

I found one new wrinkle to be particularly interesting. Fowler said investors shouldn't worry about the debt being taken on to do the deal because with copper prices at record highs, the debt could be paid down quickly. A question-worthy comment if ever I heard one!

Gary and I had prepared a few firebombs, but as it turned out, others in the room needed no help from us. To my surprise, when the Q&A session opened, Nat Jenkins took the lead on shooting down the deal.

"Jeff, we've traded in Red Metal for a long time, a decade or more, so obviously we like the stock. I'll tell you why. Red Metal has always been a good proxy for copper. When copper rose, we bought Red Metal. When it fell, we sold. And I don't mind telling you whenever copper tanked, we shorted Red Metal. As long as you're just a copper-mining company, we can figure out how to make money on your stock no matter what copper is doing.

"Now you're bringing nickel into the mix. Do nickel price cycles track with copper cycles? No. Copper shoots up early during economic expansions. Nickel doesn't kick in till much later, and usually not nearly as strong. So nickel will make it harder to trade your company. Also, it will be holding down your returns in good times. You're taking a perfectly good pure-play stock like Red Metal and complicating it. Why would you do that?"

Fowler offered the grow-or-die defense. Red Metal couldn't stand still. If it marched in place, it would lose ground against other mining companies. Combining with

NICAN and Eagle Crest would bring both greater size and increased stability to the new corporation, which would be better for everyone in the long term. Besides, most modern mining companies had diversified their metals portfolios.

"And that's why I don't own most mining companies," Nat said. "I like Red Metal just the way it is, which I would have told you if you had asked. I think my new friend David Brown here is right. You can do a lot better by us if you buy back shares or give us some hefty dividends. And you won't die. You might get acquired, but again, that would work out okay for anyone who holds your stock. We don't need this deal."

Fowler made it a point not to look my way. I made it a point to try not to look smug. I'm not sure I succeeded.

Across the room, another investor I didn't recognize stood up. Fowler knew him.

"I see we have a question from Scott Dalton at Manteso Investments. Scott?"

"Jeff, Red Metal has always been a conservative company. Your balance sheet has fallen out of whack a few times over the years, but that happened because of markets, not anything you did. Now you'll be going from practically no debt to $27 billion, and it will be because of something you did. That may work out for you, and it may not. Sure, you'll add assets, but even so, the balance sheet will be radically different, and radical is never a word I've associated with steady-as-she-goes Red Metal. What's making you do this? It's not your style."

Fowler retreated to the proud history of Red Metal. It had survived 130 years by being conservative, and acquisition, not organic growth, presented itself as the conservative step to take now. It would keep the Red Metal name, heritage and tradition alive for another 130 years.

"But it's wrong to use shareholder resources on a deal that could actually lower your return on investment and assets," Dalton said. "Are you doing this for shareholders or for yourself and your senior team? A bigger company could mean bigger paydays, right?"

Fowler kept his cool as he said he expected the new company to have stronger earnings power. He then pulled out the usual bullshit that executive pay is based on performance and set in the context of what peer companies are paying. He couldn't deny the new Red Metal NICAN would be joining a new set of larger peer companies, but the Red Metal board always demanded strong performance for strong pay. (In fairness, Fowler's compensation package at Red Metal totaled about $8 million a year, far below what my friends Don and Jerry Jack pulled down at a much smaller company.)

My friend Jim Ewald offered the next question.

"Jeff, this deal came out of nowhere, and it seems really rushed. Are you doing this just to prove you're not going to let some upstart hedge fund push you around? If so, from where I sit, this is like ginning up a tornado to blow out a match."

Fowler assured Jim the deal had been thought through thoroughly, and Red Metal made decisions with only one goal in mind—to increase shareholder value. (How many times had I heard that, from every publicly traded company in the universe? Me and everyone else in the room. Of course, I guess we all try to align ourselves on the side of virtue, no matter how seldom we actually stand there.)

After about five more questions, I rose to be recognized.

"As you know, Mr. Fowler, Galileo Capital has a few shares of Red Metal." The room broke out in polite laughter.

"Several months ago, we encouraged you to borrow money to finance a really strong buyback program. You responded—with a news release no less—that we wanted you to make a reckless bet on copper price trends. Now you're willing to make the bet, not for the few billion we had in mind but for $27 billion. What's changed?"

"Very simple, Mr. Brown. We'll be getting real assets with the money we borrow instead of just taking on debt to line your... to create a pass-through of cash to shareholders. This isn't just borrowing money to appease investors fixated on short-term gain. For what it's worth, we are feeling somewhat more confident about the foreseeable future for copper prices. But we're doing this deal for the long term.

"True to our form, we are being conservative about copper prices down the road. You know copper has been about $3.40 a pound recently. But as we've run the numbers, we've projected a copper price of just $1.75 a pound in 2008. We're not pretending these good times can last forever. Nobody should. But even at $1.75, the deal looks good.

"This deal is a real opportunity to invest for the long-term good of everyone who relies on Red Metal, shareholders included. Mr. Brown, you have to appreciate mining is different from most businesses. We make huge investments to dig holes in the ground that often have no payout. We spend billions to develop viable mines before we ever see the first pound of ore. Our timeframes are glacial, and if they don't fit yours, you might want to look for other investments.

"Red Metal is just a couple of years removed from having stared bankruptcy in the face. There are good reasons to build a company that can better navigate metal price cycles, and Red Metal NICAN will be up to the job. That will be the real change. Metal price cycles won't end, but our company will have the size and stability to weather them much better. Having held our stock for less than a year, you might not appreciate what it takes to run a business like ours."

I took a sip of water. "I believe I heard an insult somewhere in there, Mr. Fowler. I make no apologies for wanting my share of the extraordinary gains made by Red Metal during the past few years, and your ability to weather a storm is no concern of mine. I don't buy stock for any reason other than to make money for myself and my investors.

"Your timeframes may be glacial, but even so, relatively, in the blink of an eye, you've been flooded with money. More money than you know what to do with, apparently, judging by this deal. So I repeat, if you can't find a strong deal—and this isn't—then give us our money. The deal you've cut will have a hard time gaining shareholder approval. If I have to, I'll see to that myself."

I still had a couple of bites of cheesecake left, so I sat down to watch the meeting erupt into a Red Metal massacre. It ended only because Todd Williamson called time, explaining once again the Red Metal executives had to move on to their next appointment. Fowler looked as though the appointment he could use most involved a Manhattan and a punching bag.

Gary and I headed out, hearing some general murmuring about how Red Metal would have a tough time selling the Red Metal-NICAN-Eagle Crest combo. We'd walked about a block back to our office when I realized I'd left my pen at our table. You don't abandon a Montblanc without a fight, so I told Gary to head back without me while I went to retrieve it. As I returned to the Bull and Bear, the door to the private room had cracked open just a bit. Approaching from the side, I could see the wait staff scurrying about, still cleaning.

Fowler must have thought of them as deaf and dumb, or maybe he figured none of them spoke English. He didn't hesitate to create an ugly scene in front of them. He had no idea I stood outside.

"Who the fuck thought this was a good idea?" Fowler screamed at the top of his lungs as his staff remained seated with their backs to the door, shoulders sagging and heads bowed. Apparently no one wanted to make eye contact with him. "You call this a lunch? A knife fight, that's what it was, and you threw me in front of a bunch of switchblades with only a pocketknife. I'm gonna ask again: Who the fuck thought this was a good idea?"

After an interminable silence, Todd Williamson spoke.

"Jeff, you know the answer. Vassell and Hunt. You say they're the best investor relations firm in the business. They recommended having the luncheon. We took investors by surprise, so reaching out to our biggest investors soon after the announcement made sense. It let us use our time more efficiently than trying to set a dozen individual meetings around the city."

"Yeah, efficient if you're trying to get us killed in record time. If we'd met one on one, the mob mentality would never have developed. And we had to feed them fucking $200 meals too! All for the privilege of serving up ourselves as the main course. And Williamson, if you're stupid enough to defend it, you might want to start looking for another job.

"Look, I don't know how we're going to recover from this piece-of-shit meeting. But when everything clears, someone's going to call Sid Vassell and tell him our relationship with Vassell and Hunt is terminated. We've paid them a retainer for years, and just when we need them, they come up with this half-assed idea. This is bullshit!"

Just then, Fowler caught me inadvertently eavesdropping in the hallway.

"So, Brown, is this the way you do your research? Snooping around places you don't belong? We wouldn't be where we are if you hadn't decided you could jack Red Metal prices up and down on your computer. Get outta here, asshole!"

I spotted my pen and walked in to grab it. Fowler started walking toward me. I kept walking, determined not to flinch or cower. The threat vanished when a couple of his staff members caught his eye, shook their heads, and brought him to his senses.

"Mr. Fowler"—formality seemed to be in order—"I did nothing more than buy a boatload of your stock and call attention to how much money you had sitting around doing nothing. I had nothing to do with your deciding to pursue some cockamamie, two-step deal that converts your cash into questionable assets. You pushed the first domino with your Red Metal NICAN announcement. You put yourself in this mess. But you know what? I'll help you get out. As soon as I leave, I'm going to start organizing a shareholder vote against your deal. Then we'll be back at square one. And I can work on getting your company acquired. Which will suit me just fine."

With that I grabbed my pen and left, seeing the now-familiar sight of veins popping out of Jeff Fowler's neck. As I walked away, Fowler screamed at his staff to cancel the next day's luncheon in Boston.

FOURTEEN

Gary and I decided to blow off a little steam that evening. We asked Jessica and Shannon to join us for dinner and a movie. We opted for Chinese at the Tse Yang Restaurant on 51st Street just off Park Avenue. The New York Times once called the Tse Yang pricey, pretentious and meant for people who would really rather eat with forks and not be bothered by bones. A perfect recommendation, Gary and I thought, and we headed there often. Too bad it shut its doors a few years ago.

For the movie, we wanted something escapist, and *Superman Returns* fit the bill. But Jessica and Shannon pushed for *The Break-Up,* and we obliged. We'd all enjoyed Vince Vaughn in *The Wedding Crashers,* and Gary and I had nothing against Jennifer Aniston, and it took place in our hometown, Chicago, so it seemed like a good choice. As it turned out, not so much.

Vince and Jennifer (who knows what their characters' names were?) meet at a Chicago Cubs game. So far, so good. Then they buy a condo and move in together without the benefit of a wedding. No problem there.

Eventually, though, they fall victim to one of the oldest recurring arguments a couple can have: Why can't you do this one little thing for me? Why do you bring home three lemons when I asked for a dozen? Why can't you want to help me with the dishes? They push each other's buttons so much that eventually, Jennifer declares she's breaking up with Vince.

Both get stubborn about who's going to stay in the condo, so they end up living under the same roof (not the same bedroom) and find countless ways to get under each other's skin. Each makes a move toward reconciliation, but the other misses the signal. Eventually, the condo gets sold, and they move out and go their separate ways.

This being a romcom, though, there had to be a happy ending, or at least the hint of one. So at the end of the movie, they meet on the street, have a pleasant conversation and walk away from each other smiling. I keep waiting for the sequel, but so far, nothing.

Afterward, we headed to the Algonquin for drinks. Gary and I learned about the Algonquin from one of our Dominican English teachers at Fenwick, who taught a whole unit about Dorothy Parker, Robert Benchley, George Kaufman and the other literati who held forth at the Algonquin's Round Table during the Roaring Twenties. We didn't think of ourselves as particularly literary, but when Gary and I came to New York, we remembered the Algonquin, and we adopted it as our go-to bar.

The conversation rolled on without incident until Gary commented casually that none of us had the "one little thing" problem in our marriages.

"Actually, Gary," Jessica said, "I do have one little thing I wish you'd do for me more often. It's simple, really, and you should know what it is."

Oh, God, I thought. There's a trap if ever I'd seen one. Gary's not a bad guy, and I knew if he could figure out the one little thing, he would do it. And if he didn't, and guessed wrong, this evening might not end well.

"Babe, you know I'd do anything for you," he said. "Just say the word..."

"Well, if you don't know by now, you'll never know."

"I'll never know if you don't tell me! Just tell me, and I'll do it."

Thankfully, Shannon didn't play the same game with me. Instead, she tried to help Gary. Apparently, she knew what Jessica had in mind.

"Gary, I think it's something we all forget to do after a while. Just think back to the kinds of things you did when you and Jessica first met and you don't do anymore."

"Oh, so you know, do you, Shannon? What's the deal? Do you two talk about me behind my back?"

I knew the answer to that question. Don't all women? Nothing to get hung about, I concluded a long time ago. I stepped in to come to Shannon's rescue.

"Gary, I wouldn't look at it that way," I said. "Let's face it. You and I aren't always the most attentive guys around. I'm pretty sure Jessica has heard a few of my faults, and I'm glad Shannon has a place to vent. Just as long as she eventually finds a way to talk with me about it. Here's your chance to talk with Jessica about what's on her mind."

"Okay, fine. I'll do it. If you will, Jessica. But not here. Let's save this for home."

We found our way back to safer ground, had another drink, and parted ways for the night. In the cab, Shannon snuggled up next to me.

"So what is it Jessica wants Gary to do for her?"

"Snuggle, just like we're snuggling now."

"Is that all? I thought it would be something expensive, knowing Jessica."

"Hmm. She's my best friend, you know. I should be pissed."

"But you're not, right?"

"No, I know her too well. I see why you say that."

"You mind if I tell Gary tomorrow, just in case he doesn't find out tonight?"

"No, be my guest. I hate to see him flounder about for too long. Just give him a few pointers on how not to be obvious about how he figured it out."

"Yeah, okay. You know, Gary and I really wanted to see *Superman Returns*. Looking back, it seems like it would have been a safer choice. These couples movies always scare a guy, you know."

"Tell you what. When we get home, let's do our own version of *Superman Returns*. You can be Superman."

"Hey, we can take turns!"

She laughed. I smiled and pulled her closer to me. That night, Superman returned, several times.

• • •

The next morning, I walked to our offices in the Chrysler Building. It's about two and half miles from our place, but I had the time, and I wanted the exercise.

Late June in New York can be brutal—hot and sticky. That day, however, I found to be tolerable; a light drizzle drove the humidity high, but the temperature reached a high of only 75.

I needed an umbrella, and I make it a point to buy one on the street whenever I can. The vendors charge only $5. If they're willing to hustle for a buck, I'm happy to support them. Then, once a year or so, Shannon and I throw the umbrellas in with other stuff we wanted to dump and cab everything over to the Goodwill store a half mile from us on Second

Avenue. We valued the umbrellas at $15 apiece and take a tax write-off. So really, I pick up the umbrellas practically for free and help out somebody to boot. You gotta love America, right?

Whenever I walk the streets of the city alone, I find myself wondering about all the people around me. Are they native New Yorkers, and if not, how did they come to be here? Which ones are successful? Which ones are faking it until they make it? Which ones have given up caring whether they succeed or not? On this particular walk, I thought back to a trip I'd taken several years before on the Staten Island Ferry.

In between my second and third marriages—a socially aimless time for me—I'd ride the ferry at least one weekend a month, usually late at night. I'd catch the 10 o'clock departure on the Manhattan side then come back on the 11:30 trip from Staten Island.

The ferry has always been one of the best deals in town, and in 1997, the city decided to make each trip, every day, totally free. Rudy Giuliani and the Metropolitan Transit Authority eliminated ferry fares when they instituted free transfers within the five-borough transit system. New York pundits hailed and cursed eliminating the fare as a great election-year gift to all Staten Islanders, some of Giuliani's strongest supporters. But I'm sure he never even thought of any political payoff from the move. Right.

I didn't care what the ferry cost, of course. I loved the late-night quietness, the isolation, the spectacular views of the Statue of Liberty, and the snack bar's beer and kraut dogs with mustard. The trips gave me a chance to see a slice of humanity I never experience any more. And on the rare occasions I wanted to indulge in "unlucky in love" pity, the trips allowed me to wallow in the loneliness that can be so overwhelming in a city of 8½ million people.

One Saturday night, on the trip over to Staten Island, I shared the main, enclosed deck with four other guys. I sat a couple of seats back from them, but I could hear every word they said as I chewed through my kraut dog and guzzled my beer.

It seemed three of them worked as Catholic grade school teachers on Staten Island, and they had just had a night on the town in Manhattan, doing whatever Catholic grade school teachers do to party down. The fourth—a stranger to them, it turned out—struck up a conversation in a hurry. Like he wanted an audience. They all appeared to be in their late 20s.

The fourth announced he had been a lawyer at Graham and Trafalgar, one of the city's oldest, silk-stocking firms, for a year. At his age, he had to be just another young law graduate on a hamster wheel, putting in his 90 hours a week chasing the partnership dangled in front of him. His slur—slight, but a slur nonetheless—revealed he had decided to indulge in a couple of drinks after yet another long Saturday at the office. He had the Brooks Brothers look and demeanor. His salary didn't yet permit him to live in Manhattan, but as things developed, we all heard he'd soon be moving up.

He asked where his three travel companions hailed from, originally. (A New Yorker can easily sniff out non-natives.) Like me, they all came from the Midwest, two from Wisconsin and one from St. Louis. None of them had lived in New York for more than three years. Marshalls appeared to be their high-end clothing store of choice. The lawyer grimaced when they told him what they did.

"Let me tell you what I think about you guys," he said. "You might find it useful. I've lived here all my life. Went to Staten Island Academy from K to 12, which as you might know is the best school on the island. It opened the door for me to NYU and then Columbia Law School. I worked for years to get off the island, and my parents drove into my head how important that is. I live here now because some buddies and I room together, but we're making the move to Manhattan next month.

"Here's what I think you guys need to know. This city has one word for you—losers. You're not going to make it here. Sooner or later, you'll get chewed up, thrown out and shipped to the landfill, which, conveniently enough, is on the Island. This is no place for guys like you. You should leave while the leaving's good."

The tallest of the three—pudgy, bespectacled and oozing Midwest earnestness—became their spokesman. He said they didn't get into their line of work for the money, but they made enough to be comfortable. They'd each gone to Catholic schools (like me), and they'd each chosen being part of a Catholic school as something worthwhile to do with their lives. They'd all come to Staten Island by way of Marquette University, and they liked doing what they did. They had a decent parish on the island, and they enjoyed being part of the city. Besides, there's lots of things to do that don't cost a cent.

"And I don't want to spend the rest of my life doing them," the young lawyer said. "Living on Staten Island is not being part of the city. Trust me. You'll get tired of this, and you'll go back home. And when you do, you'll know you're losers. If you stay, let's see what comfort your God gives you years from now, when you're living on food stamps in some fleabag apartment."

The conversation, if you could call it that, ended there. The Catholics didn't protest, and the lawyer walked away to stand outside and let the wind wash over him. The harbor breeze can sometimes hasten a sobering.

I kept my mouth shut. I had some sympathy for the Catholic guys. After all, we all went through Catholic schools. But I knew I'd made the same choice as the lawyer. The Fenwick priests tried to sell guys like me and Gary on the service spiel, but we didn't bite.

During my walk to the office, I realized I could be nearly as judgmental as the lawyer on the ferry. The question I asked about each person who passed me boiled down to, "Loser? Or no loser?" And as I approached our office, I rejoiced because I wasn't a loser. And God knows the lawyer's arrogance appalled me, so I was a good guy, right? I had no regrets about the path I had chosen.

●　●　●

Gary and I wanted the Chrysler Building for our offices because we're both architecture buffs—again, the Frank Lloyd Wright legacy from Oak Park—and we considered the Chrysler Building to be the most beautiful in Manhattan. The Empire State Building gets more buzz, but really, there's no comparison.

Don't get me wrong. Modern architects throw up boxes that shirk beauty to maximize space, so the Empire State Building is much better than anything being built today in New York. But most of it came off the rack. Many of its components, such as doors and windows, could be ordered from building supply catalogs of the day.

By comparison, the Chrysler Building is a work of fine sculpture. You can't beat the flush windows, the stainless steel crown, and the spire sitting atop the building. Both buildings are Art Deco structures, but the Chrysler Building, with its unique, automobile-inspired, radiator-cap and hood-ornament gargoyles; its lobby of blood-red Moroccan marble and sienna travertine capped by Edward Turnbull's ceiling mural tribute to American ingenuity and industriousness; and its white and gray brick façade, is unparalleled on this planet. We wanted to be there. Management offered us a 3,500-square-foot space at a great price, $50 a square foot, so we signed a 10-year lease.

My walk to the office took about 45 minutes—east on 86th Street and then south on Lexington. I ran into Gary when I emerged from the elevator on the 25th floor.

"Everything go okay last night?"

He said he and Jessica were copacetic. She just wanted Gary to snuggle more, he learned, so he made it happen... which led to an hour or so of more strenuous physical activity. (At least, according to Gary. I'm guessing more like 20 minutes. Guys exaggerate, you know?)

"So that's squared away." He smiled. "Meantime, the plot thickens on Red Metal. I learned this morning Fowler and company have engaged Smithington as their proxy solicitors. Maybe we should think about hiring someone to solicit for us."

Smithington is the oldest, biggest proxy solicitation firm in the United States, and it had grown geometrically since the 1980s. Until then, most annual meetings and special shareholder meetings shook out as quiet little gatherings with a few, mundane, legally required items to vote on, some patter from the CEO about earnings and outlook, and some decent *hors d'oeuvres* for the sparse crowd in attendance.

Often, many of the seats at an annual meeting would go unused. A company's retirees would be the bulk of the attendees. They'd use the meeting as a mini-reunion, a chance to make sure the company had their pension fund in good hands, and an opportunity to enjoy some tasty snacks. Beginning in the 1980s, activist shareholders turned many annual meetings into titanic battles, setting the stage for companies like Smithington to grow. I'll tell you more about what they do in a moment.

To be sure, there had been some activist activity early in the 20th century. In 1916, for example, Henry Ford, after accumulating a capital surplus of $60 million, declared he would cancel a special dividend to shareholders. Instead, he planned to use the money to expand production and increase the number of people he employed. His reason? "My ambition is to employ still more men, to spread the benefits of this industrial system to the greatest possible number, to help them build their lives and their homes. To do this, we are putting our greatest share of our profits back in the business."

Noble sentiments, but sullied by greed. In reality, Ford wanted to keep the dividend away from fellow shareholders John Francis Dodge and Horace Elgin Dodge, who owned about 10 percent of the company. Ford suspected the Dodge brothers wanted to use their dividend to help build a rival car company, and the brothers proved him right. Next time you see a Viper or a Charger rolling down the street, know it has a little bit of Ford blood coursing through its veins, rightfully siphoned away as cash by those early shareholder activists, the Dodge brothers.

To get their dividend, the brothers sued, and in 1919, the Michigan Supreme Court ordered Ford to pay out an extra dividend of $19.3 million. Galileo Capital holds the words of the ruling in reverence. We framed them and hung them in our foyer. Every hedge fund should.

"A business corporation is organized and carried on primarily for the profit of the stockholders. The powers of the directors are to be employed for that end. The direction of directors is to be exercised in the choice of means to attain that end, and does not extend to a change in the end itself, to the reduction of profits, or to the non-distribution of profits among stockholders in order to devote them to other purposes."

Activist activity waned during most of the rest of the 20th century. The Great Depression and World War II kept people preoccupied for long stretches of time, and an unprecedented period of growth in the post-war period kept most shareholders both sanguine and docile.

By the 1980s, however, American greed reawakened, and annual meetings (and the votes that had to be taken) became danger zones for corporations. Carl Icahn—a personal hero of mine—led a hostile takeover of TWA in 1985. T. Boone Pickens wreaked havoc in the oil and gas industry.

A decade later, the mushrooming of executive pay stimulated a new wave of shareholder activists. Since the late 1990s—when Galileo Capital came into being—there are five primary avenues of attack against corporations:

1. **Underperformance.** If a company is underperforming its peers or the general market, you can bet some activist is looking to knock on the door. This is the vulnerability we used against Mangelsdorf Pharmaceuticals.

2. **Corporate clarity.** This line of attack argues shareholders would be better served if businesses unrelated or only loosely related to one another each stood on their own. Each spinoff theoretically unlocks value and lets the new entity be more focused on its mission and markets.

3. Governance. If a board is too cozy with management, or can't be changed quickly through a vote, or is structured to make it difficult for shareholders to effect change, a shareholder activist could be inspired to make a run at the company. Usually, if executive pay seems excessive, the problem can be traced back to a governance issue. Jerry Jack and Don, for example, probably had a lot of personal friends on their board.

4. Corporate control. Shareholders can be riled up if they believe a company should receive more for a proposed sale, or should abandon a proposed acquisition, or should put itself up for sale to create more value.

5. Capital allocation. If a company is swimming in cash, it's liable to be hounded to use it productively or give back money to shareholders with dividends or share buybacks.

The last two should sound familiar. Red Metal heard No. 5 from us constantly, and No. 4 quickly came into play once the company proposed creating Red Metal NICAN.

Not long after a company comes under attack, or shortly after it senses it might be vulnerable, it usually seeks out a proxy solicitation firm. Red Metal chose Smithington.

The quixotic mission for Smithington? Generate a favorable vote for the company's convoluted deal. Because of the shellacking he took at the New York luncheon, Fowler knew his deal had its detractors. He probably believed, though—because of personal pride if for no other reason— that most shareholders would vote to support the Red Metal-NICAN-Eagle Crest deal. And just as a politician needs to turn out all his favorable voters on Election Day, so Fowler wanted to make sure his sympathetic shareholders exercised their right to vote. If apathy set in, and they failed to cast their votes, for whatever reason, the activists—in this case, Galileo and our allies—might win.

Smithington, as the biggest proxy solicitation firm, had both relationships and efficient systems in place to call shareholders and ask them to let Smithington vote their proxy in favor of the deal. They made such calls often, on behalf of many clients, and because institutional investors held nearly 80 percent of Red Metal stock, somewhere between 300 and 500 calls would let them know quickly where the deal stood. If a call headed south, Smithington had more latitude than Red Metal to discuss whether the deal might be modified to make it acceptable to a shareholder.

Funny thing. They never called us.

Gary and I discussed his idea of hiring our own proxy solicitation firm. After all, I had threatened Fowler with doing so, and it would have been fun to get under his skin when word spread that we, too, had started soliciting proxies. We decided, however, to wait a few weeks to see how things would unfold. The shareholder vote probably wouldn't be scheduled for a few months, and in the meantime, we could get a reasonable sense of the direction of things just by talking with a few of our fellow investors. No sense spending money if we didn't have to.

FIFTEEN

The day after July 4 (another of the countless holidays for the feds), I received a call from Agents Katz and Hardaway saying they'd be coming around in a couple of days to look for more documents. They also wanted to check for evidence about whether we might have destroyed any records since their last visit. We hadn't, of course. It seemed like a good time to trade on our information about Dennis Clobes.

After talking it over more with Gary and Ben Becker, and our lawyer, Peter Barrows, I saw no reason to involve Fowler. Whether he had asked Clobes to do him a favor or not, he had no power to call off the investigation. Only Clobes could make that happen.

Early on July 6, I took a cab to 200 Vesey Street, armed with a photo of Clobes from Ben Becker. I spotted him coming from the subway, carrying a Starbucks cup in one hand and a briefcase in another. Like Fowler, he looked as though he had once played offensive line. Unlike Fowler, much of his muscle had turned to flab.

"Dennis Clobes? Let me introduce myself. We have a mutual acquaintance in Jeff Fowler."

He smiled, and his eyes lit up.

"Is that right? Jeff is one of my best friends. How do you know him?"

"We've had some business dealings, and I spent some time with him last year in Arizona. I'm David Brown."

It took him a few seconds, but when he placed the name, he scowled.

"Mr. Brown, I don't have conversations with people who are under investigation. I have reason to believe you've been involved with some shady dealings in Red Metal stock. I have nothing to say to you. Please leave me, and I mean now."

The truth is, I said, everything we've done around Red Metal—and every other investment we make—is done by the book. There's no evidence to the contrary, and we did nothing to provoke an investigation.

"What exactly led you to believe you had something on us? A tip? A study of our public filings? Odd trading patterns?"

Silence on Clobes's end.

"Just as I thought, nothing! My guess is Fowler put you up to this, or more likely, you wanted to do a favor for a friend. Okay, so here's what's going to happen. First, I want you to call off Katz and Hardaway from any more visits to our office. Second, I want you to announce within a week—and not at the end of the day Friday, when news releases go to die—that Galileo has been cleared of any wrongdoing in regard to Red Metal stock or any other transactions."

"I certainly will not! You're in no position to dictate to me or the SEC or the FBI how your case will be handled."

"If it doesn't happen, I'll start proceedings against you and the SEC. I'll tell the world about how you and your buddy Fowler played football together and how you're still tight today. I'll say you knowingly abused your power to harass Galileo and alienate our investors from us. I'll take the story to the media too, and you can spend a couple of weeks with your boss explaining exactly why you came after us. And with your lawyers and PR people trying to decide how to respond to our blitz. You don't want that, and I'm not sure your buddy Jeff wants so much controversy spinning around when he's trying to pull off the deal of his life. Which, like this little fishing expedition you have going against Galileo, will also go nowhere."

Clobes stormed away, feigning outrage, but the way his coffee cup shook showed I had rattled him. Katz and Hardaway never showed up. Six days later—not a moment too soon for him—a news release went out from the SEC announcing we had been cleared. A highly unusual step, I believe.

I got an avalanche of media calls asking how it felt to have our SEC investigation called off. "Absolutely delightful," I said. "There's nothing better than being given a clean bill of health after the FBI and the SEC pay you a visit."

Gradually, the investors who left us started coming back.

•　　•　　•

July turned out to be a good month for us but an ugly month for Jeff Fowler. Galileo, we liked to believe, caused many sleepless nights for him, but we had plenty of comrades in arms during the heart of the summer.

Red Metal apparently hadn't reckoned on good old, red-blooded (or however they'd say it) Canadian nationalism. For most of a century, mining has been nearly invisible in the United States. History books are full of stories both tragic and romantic about coal mine collapses, gold rushes and miners' strikes. Day to day, though, unless you live in West Virginia, Arizona, Nevada or a handful of other states, chances are good you know little about miners and mining, which accounts for only two percent of the U.S. gross domestic product, or about $300 billion.

Mining is near the bottom of the list of major industry sectors, far below real estate, durable manufacturing and nondurable manufacturing. Agriculture brings up the rear, which may be why miners and farmers have an affinity for each other. They're both fond of saying all wealth begins either with mining or farming. "If it can't be grown, it must be mined" is a saying both groups use to remind the world they are responsible for all the raw materials needed to make everything from clothes to computer chips.

In Canada, mining is a much bigger deal, accounting for about eight percent of the gross domestic product. It consistently ranks in the top three or four economic sectors. Simply put, mining is a superstar industry.

Now, think back to how you felt a couple of decades ago when Japanese firms started buying big U.S. companies in high-profile industries. Does it still stick in your craw that Sony owns Columbia Pictures? Apparently that's how Canadians felt when they heard a foreign company wanted to cut a deal to buy NICAN and Eagle Crest. It especially pissed them off that the company was based in the U.S.

We see Canadians as rational, polite and self-effacing. True enough. But there is a streak of resentment toward the U.S. You can hear it in their jokes. For example:

> On the sixth day God turned to the Archangel Gabriel and said: "Today I am going to create a land called Canada. It will be a land of outstanding natural beauty. It shall have tall majestic mountains full of bears and eagles, beautifully sparkling lakes bountiful with trout, forests full of elk and moose, high cliffs overlooking sandy beaches with an abundance of sea life, and rivers stocked with salmon."

God continued, *"I shall make the land rich in oil so the inhabitants will prosper. I shall call these inhabitants 'Canadians,' and they shall be known as the friendliest people on the earth."*

"But, Lord," said Gabriel, "don't you think you are being too generous to these Canadians?"

"Not really," replied God. "Just wait and see the neighbors I'm going to give them."

Or this one:

How many U.S. tourists does it take to change a light bulb?

Fifteen. Five to figure out how much the bulb costs in the local currency, four to comment on "how funny-looking" local lightbulbs are, three to hire a local person to change the bulb, two to take pictures, and one to buy postcards in case the pictures don't come out.

When the news spread about Red Metal's cutting a deal with NICAN and Eagle Crest, the Canadian outrage soon followed. Within a week, the chairman of Canada's Holman Gold Corp., Paul Szabo, was granting interviews to any media outlet that asked, calling the deal "irrational" and saying it provided no net benefit to Canada.

Szabo, who fled Hungary with his parents to avoid Jewish persecution during World War II, became a naturalized, renowned Canadian entrepreneur, businessman and philanthropist. His opinion carried weight, or at least received generous coverage.

Recall that when he announced the deal, Fowler made a point of noting it would produce a "net benefit" to Canada. As I said, attorneys probably shoehorned those words into the remarks.

Under the Investment Canada Act, adopted in 1985, all major foreign investments in the country are subject to approval by the federal government. A reviewable investment must pass the test of providing a net benefit to the country. Six different dimensions are considered:

1. The effect on economic activity in Canada.

2. The degree of participation by Canadians in the business to be created or modified.

3. The effect of the investment on productivity, efficiency, technological development, product innovation and product variety in Canada.

4. The effect of the investment on competition.

5. The compatibility of the investment with national industrial, economic and cultural policies.

6. The contribution to Canada's ability to compete globally.

Szabo said he had talked to "many people" about the deal, and no one could cite a major Canadian interest that would be served. He saw leaving some corporate jobs in Toronto as a cheap PR ploy. He stopped short, however, of saying the deal should be disallowed. Instead, he encouraged the government to drag its feet in making a ruling. "No sense looking protectionist when a better deal probably will be made within the country's borders," he said.

You'll recall another Canadian company, Hecht Komando, also wanted NICAN. Szabo predicted that eventually, Red Metal's shareholders would reject its proposed deal, and Hecht and NICAN would find a way to come together. As for Eagle Crest, Szabo thought Extracta, which already owned 20 percent of Eagle Crest, would prevail in its bid, and Hecht Komando might cut a deal to achieve significant efficiencies by managing the Eagle Crest operations in Sudbury. Time would tell, of course. Szabo never addressed why it would be okay for Extracta, a Swiss company, to buy Eagle Crest but unacceptable for a U.S. company to buy NICAN. My guess is it just didn't feel right to have the Big Brother from the South in position to start barking orders to its little brother up north.

For the most part, Szabo kept his comments strictly professional. But in at least two interviews I read, he offered this jab: "As for Fowler, I doubt he can even tell the difference between nickel and tin."

"Man, that's snide," Gary said. And then we laughed. Often.

About mid-July, Fowler and a small contingent of Red Metal executives traveled on a goodwill mission to Sudbury, a city of about 160,000 in the heart of nickel country. Red Metal projected $550 million in savings could be found by completing the NICAN-Eagle Crest merger, and the Sudbury operations accounted for much of this. The deal, if completed, would turn about 8,000 NICAN and Eagle Crest employees in Sudbury into Red Metal NICAN employees.

According to the Sudbury Times, Fowler kicked off his tour with a Friday night dinner for 100 community leaders. He and his team then spent the weekend visiting mining towns in the region, trying to meet as many employees, retirees and suppliers as possible. Not knowing Fowler to be an outgoing, gregarious guy, I took this as a sign of desperation to drum up some support for his deal.

"One of the challenges right now is to be in 30 places at once and still get some sleep," he told the Times. "I understand, though. A lot of people will be affected by this deal, and they have lots of questions. We're determined to make the people of Sudbury as comfortable as they can be." Unfortunately for Fowler, the Times and other media didn't exactly fall in line to make anyone comfortable.

One strain of reporting questioned whether Red Metal would stay as committed to corporate philanthropy as Eagle Crest and, particularly, NICAN had proved to be. Over the years, NICAN had become known as "Mother NICAN" in Sudbury because of all it contributed to community causes (not to mention being such a large employer). "Now," one dignitary said, "Mother is marrying an unknown company who will become our stepfather and who has other kids in the U.S., Peru, Chile, and other countries worldwide. Will the stepfather love them more than us? Will they get more handed over to their community causes? The best we can do is wait and see."

Another spate of stories questioned the strength of Red Metal's commitment to environmental responsibility. "A couple of years ago, the company dropped its membership in the International Council on Mining and Metals, and it has never published a corporate responsibility report," one editorial said. "How committed can it be to the environment if it can't even be bothered to issue a report?"

At least Red Metal had saved a few trees, I thought, by not publishing a report that almost no one reads. Stick it on a website, for God's sake. Seriously, though, the criticism about Red Metal's lack of commitment to corporate responsibility had to be liberal whining, or "boo hoo from the blue," as I called it.

If anything, from my viewpoint, the company in recent years had sunk too much money into the corporate responsibility crap. Fowler and friends couldn't figure out what else to do with the flood of cash washing over them, so they poured 50 million new bucks into their foundation. They sank $1 billion—$1 billion!—into fully funding their pension program. (Carl Icahn probably threw up when he heard.) They set up a $500 million trust fund to protect air, soil and water at their operating sites. And they committed to spending $150 million to clean up pollution at "legacy" operations, which no longer produce copper but still carry a shitload of environmental issues.

As an investor, I liked seeing Red Metal get their environmental issues accounted for with real, hard cash. That's much better than waiting for fines and lawsuits from the EPA, state governments and other countries. It helps reduce uncertainty about the future. But shit—more than $1.5 billion squirreled away without any immediate, tangible return? With that money, the people in the town of Mordecai might get to see their kids put on some lame production of *Oklahoma!*, but it wouldn't do much for us shareholders.

July closed on a sour note for Red Metal investors. When Red Metal announced its second-quarter earnings, it said its copper-collar initiative had reduced second-quarter income by nearly $515 million! Is it any wonder Gary and I characterized the company as "undermanaged"?

SIXTEEN

As Fowler made the rounds in Sudbury, Shannon and I had visitors. First, my mom called, asking whether I could get good seats for *Jersey Boys*, the hot Broadway ticket. I told her to come on out and we'd see it. Then Shannon received a call from Janis Fowler. With her husband swamped night and day by the NICAN deal, she had decided to spend a couple of weeks in the Big Apple, and she'd love to see Shannon. "No sense letting a little squabble between our men get in the way of our getting together," she said.

I couldn't believe Fowler would approve of this. I know I didn't. But no one sought my approval—or Fowler's, I imagine—and I saw no way to protest the arrangement. I could've said their getting together could be seen as collusion, but I guessed Janis had as little interest as Shannon in the game between Fowler and me. If the SEC got wind of their time together, Janis and Shannon would rightfully point out neither of them had any interest or legal standing in the matter. So I bit my tongue and decided to look big about the whole situation. Until Shannon said we should take Janis to *Jersey Boys* too.

"Shannon! I can tolerate your getting together with her, even though it'll drive me nuts! Go do what you want, but don't ask me to get involved. Besides, my mom wants to be with us, not with some stranger. And after a drink or two, who knows what I might end up saying or what Janis might end up saying. Fowler might even be putting her up to all this, now that I think about it. Get us together, have a drink or two, and who knows what might come out of my mouth! If I say the wrong thing, and she tells Fowler, who knows what could happen?"

Shannon said my mom would love meeting Janis, they're both salt of the earth. And they came of age when the Four Seasons dominated the charts. And I probably owed Janis a nice evening, seeing as how she made it possible for me to tour the Mordecai mine. And if I worried about what I might say after a drink or two, then I should just stick with Coke for the evening.

Deep down, I had to agree my mom would probably enjoy meeting Janis. They both exuded graciousness. Just as Janis found a way to douse the anger that flared up between Fowler and me at Durant's, my mom had established a good record as an effective peacemaker.

When Gary and I entered Fenwick High, my dad had already died. He began his career as a meat cutter in Chicago's Union Stockyards but moved to a local Dominick's grocery store in Oak Park in the early '60s. I remember clearly he had a couple of fingers, one on each hand, that fell an inch or two shorter than they should have—a hazard of the trade, he used to say. He loved to laugh, and he loved red meat, beer, and cigarettes in an era not well-informed about moderation. One day, when I came home from seventh grade, my mother told me she found him in the bathroom, dead of a heart attack. By the time I made it to high school, she had adjusted well to being a widow. She never remarried, so I came to think of myself as the man of the family. It's one thing that fueled my ambition.

Our senior year, the Mothers Club, a hotbed of political intrigue, elected Mom president. Mom really had no idea of the quagmire she faced, but she owned Ann Brown's Card and Stationery Shop on Lake Street in Oak Park—not far from the Wright-designed Unity Temple—and she thought it would be good for business.

She learned too late that three times in the previous five years, Mothers Club presidents had stepped down early. It turned out a small clique of mothers, with multiple sons coming through Fenwick over a 10- to 12-year period, ran the club without actually holding any offices. They made it their business to "suggest" venues for dances, activities for fundraisers, and even which "mother mentors" should be assigned to the mothers of incoming freshmen. Not earth-shattering issues, but it can be annoying as hell when you're supposed to be in charge and busybodies keep second-guessing you all the time.

Most mothers didn't mind paying their monthly dues, but they rarely showed up at meetings, which meant the small, "mean moms" cadre controlled the votes on key issues. None of them wanted to hold office; they avoided the headaches and the time drain to coordinate with the administration, recruit business owners to support activities, and do all the other tasks that keep a small, volunteer organization running. They found it easier to elect some noble but unsuspecting patsies to do those things and then set the agenda with their often contrary votes.

Mom's predecessors had simply quit once they discerned their patsy status, leaving some hapless vice president to suffer through to the bitter end of the school year. Mom, however, frustrated though she was, decided she wouldn't let anybody drum her out.

She considered head-on confrontation but wrote it off, figuring she had no real power to coerce or retaliate against the mean moms. Instead, she changed the meeting time from Tuesday evenings to Saturday mornings to make it easier for more mothers to attend. Then she sent out a mailing to offer a free gift and a 10 percent discount at her shop for each time a mother came to a meeting. These changes worked, and she created an engaged, more supportive group to help get her initiatives approved, peacefully and without ugliness. She wrote off the giveaways as in-kind contributions to Fenwick (which is where I learned my Goodwill umbrella trick).

I weighed my options and saw no way to keep Shannon happy without agreeing to a trip to Jersey Boys with three feisty women. Frankie Valli's advice would have been to walk like a man, but sometimes you have to crawl like a worm to make a relationship work.

Outside the August Wilson Theatre, mom and Janis hit it off immediately, especially after Janis complimented her on raising such an accomplished son and having such a wonderful daughter-in-law. Her eyes lit up immediately, and in the corner of my eye, I could see Shannon giving me her "I told you so" look.

Mom came late to high life in Manhattan, but she knew the ropes after spending lots of time with Shannon and me. She asked if we'd all be ok with going to Sardi's after the show.

"I dreamed of going to Sardi's as a young girl on Staten Island," Janis said. "I've been there many times since, but I never get tired of it. Yes, great idea, Ann!"

I ended up identifying with Valli and his Jersey Boys. My Fenwick high-school buddies and I never bounced in and out of prison for petty crimes as the Four Seasons had, but I'd done a shady thing or two early in my career. I didn't condemn the Four Seasons; they just sinned differently from how I do.

We had a lot in common. We all came from modest beginnings. We developed the talents we had. We met a few people who helped us. Mainly, though, we had to wheel and deal our ways to the top of our respective heaps, and we had to keep performing to stay there. They hit it big during my mom and Janis's teenage years, but their story is eternal.

After the show, Janis suggested we walk to Sardi's through Times Square. "For me, there's no quicker way to get plugged into the spirit of the city than to walk down Broadway," she explained. And no quicker way to get panhandled, I thought. Which happened. I gladly did business with umbrella salesmen on the city streets, but Shannon and I had become hardened years earlier to the pleas of New York City's beggars. They seemed to me to be running an all-cash business and making a living tax free. Mom and Janis, though, responded generously, throwing dollars and coins in cups along the way. Sweet but naïve, I thought.

Once inside Sardi's, we all decided to eat light. Shannon and I split a chicken club sandwich. Mom and Janis each opted for the onion soup.

The caricatures on the walls made small talk easy. My mom and Janis bonded over drawings of their favorite TV stars. Dick Van Dyke, Mary Tyler Moore, Bob Hope, Carol Burnett and Danny Thomas, among others, kept them talking for a good 20 minutes or so. Shannon and I had our own favorites from later generations—John Stamos, Rosie Perez, James Spader, Martin Short, and Rita Wilson.

"We're being really rude," Janis suddenly said. "I want to spend some time talking with you kids. No business, though, okay? Jeff would shoot me if he thought we would sort through all his carryings-on up in Canada. Let's just let it lie."

"Fine with us!" Shannon said. She proceeded to tell my mom about her day in Sedona with Janis and how she thought my mom and Janis had a lot in common. A Staten Islander and an Oak Park native should, she said—both middle class, both well grounded, both religious.

Janis laughed. "Well, I may have strayed from my religious roots a bit. There's not a lot of fervor for religion in Arizona. But Jeff and I make it to church once in a while. Actually, I feel like I do the most good not through church but through our family foundation."

I hadn't heard anything from Shannon about family foundations since our flight back from Phoenix the previous November. I'd never even thought about the topic coming up. I wished we could talk about Fowler's NICAN deal instead of this. My mom wanted to hear more.

Janis said she and Fowler put in an initial $5 million, and they invested it conservatively so it generates five to eight percent return a year. They never use more than four percent of the funds in any given year, so they have about $200,000 a year for contributions. They use the foundation in part to support causes they care about and in part to teach their children about the importance of giving back to the community.

My mom turned to me. "So, David, your dad would be thrilled to see your success, and he'd be even more thrilled to see you create a Brown Family Foundation. Have you ever thought about starting one yourself?"

Before I could answer, Shannon chimed in.

"Actually, Ann, David and I have been talking about it. We don't have kids to inspire, of course, but I have an interest in running a foundation, and I have some thoughts about the types of causes we could support."

Mom said with as few obligations as we had, starting a foundation would be a wonderful idea. Then she asked what types of causes Shannon would care about.

"Because of how my mother died, I'd really like to support causes that work to reduce maternal mortality. The truth is, it's not a large problem in the United States. But worldwide, one woman dies about every 90 seconds because of complications during pregnancy or childbirth. I'd love to do something to help. For David, we haven't talked about anything specifically, but I know he loves architecture. I think we could find several organizations that support good architecture and architectural education in this country."

This started to feel like an ambush. I really didn't want to get into the foundation business, but I couldn't quite put my finger on why. Was I really just a selfish jerk?

Mom tried to push me for a commitment on the spot, but I retreated to my position of "let's study this and decide later." Mom winked at Shannon.

"David, I think you might just be putting off the inevitable. When I come back at Christmas, I'm thinking the Brown Family Foundation would be a great present."

While I mulled all this over, the three women made plans to take the Circle Line boat tour around Manhattan. We closed out the bill and grabbed a cab, taking a slight detour to drop Janis at the Waldorf before heading home.

After Mom went to bed, I shook my head at Shannon and then broke out laughing.

"Well played," I said. "How long have you been hatching this foundation conversation in front of my mother?"

Shannon looked truly hurt and said it all had unfolded naturally. After all, Janis brought up her foundation unprompted. Nobody forced the topic into the conversation.

"But what's the deal, anyway? Why are you so concerned about putting a few million into a family foundation? It's not like we'll ever even miss it." She had a point.

As nearly as I could tell, my ego kept me from warming up to the idea. Siphoning off even a few million from everything we had felt like I'd be shrinking, like I'd be less of a man.

"Some guys have Corvettes, you have your bank account," Shannon said. "Can't you see that's totally irrational?"

It was, I admitted.

"If anything, most people will see you as more of a man, not less. If that's what's holding you back, get over it! It's time we started giving back in a big way. God knows we can."

"All right. I'm warming up to the idea. But if we're going to do this, let's pony up $10 million to start. At least let me have the pleasure of having a bigger foundation than Fowler's!"

Gladly, Shannon said. I guess I showed her!

Then she disappeared for a few minutes. Next time I saw her, she stood naked just inside the bedroom door, holding two champagne flutes in one hand and a bottle of champagne in the other. "Come on in. Let's celebrate!"

SEVENTEEN

By mid-to-late July, Fowler's bad press in Canada had to have been moving toward the bottom of his worry list. He must have been far more troubled by seeing his Rubik's Cube of a deal falling apart.

Extracta, which already owned 20 percent of Eagle Crest, announced an increase in its bid for Eagle Crest by 12 percent to about $14.4 billion, or $53.10 a share. On paper, the Red Metal-NICAN offer factored out better at $54.90 for each Eagle Crest share. Remember, though, Red Metal NICAN's offer consisted of a combination of stock and cash, and just a few weeks earlier, before downward movement in Red Metal's stock price, the Red Metal NICAN offer equated to $57.60 a share. Extracta would give investors hard cash for each share of Eagle Crest stock.

As an investor, a cash offer attracts me more than one whose value fluctuates day to day with market ups and downs. Fowler had to know investors would see it my way, and it had to worry him.

Also, rumors ran rampant that, in addition to Hecht Komando, other companies would take a run at NICAN and separately at Eagle Crest. Just to add a little more spice to the stew, reports began circulating that several companies had been eyeing Red Metal as a takeover target.

Gary and I, of course, loved all the commotion. We celebrated anything keeping Red Metal from a clear path to its two-step acquisition, and it seemed as though we celebrated almost every day.

Not long after the Extracta announcement, my admin, Beth, told me to pick up the phone for Mike, our Phoenix limo driver.

"Good to hear your voice, Mike," I said. "What's up?"

"Just thought you'd want to know I had Fowler in my limo a few minutes ago. He called somebody on his cell phone, blasting you with names I'd blush to repeat to a Longshoreman. He talked a lot about things happening in Canada. I've taken an interest since I met you, so I've been following things in the news.

"Anyway, he told the guy on the other end that the American government won't oppose the deal he's trying to pull off. He and his people face a new question now about whether to put any more cash on the table to make it happen."

"I'll be surprised if they don't. They have to make NICAN's offer for Eagle Crest competitive. If they can't pick up Eagle Crest, there's not really much reason for the rest of the deal to go through."

Mike said he really didn't understand all the ins and outs of the deal.

I laughed. "Don't worry about it! Even sophisticated investors are having trouble figuring out why it would make any sense. No reason you should."

I thanked him for calling and promised I'd make it worth his while. He told me he'd keep his ears open for anything interesting.

Just after market close, Red Metal issued a news release. The U.S. Department of Justice and the U.S. Federal Trade Commission had granted early termination of the waiting period under the Hart-Scott-Rodino Antitrust Agreements of 1976 relating to Red Metal's acquisition of NICAN. Mike's information proved to be right, so apparently the next announcement probably would be Red Metal's sweetening of the offer for NICAN and, by extension, NICAN's sweetening of its offer for Eagle Crest.

Less than a week later, the announcement came. Red Metal's new offer worked out to $72.63 for NICAN—$18.25 cash—which would give NICAN enough to increase its bid for Eagle Crest to $57.10 with a cash component of $26.73. In addition, Eagle Crest said it would fatten the offer with a special dividend of 67 cents a share.

To a novice investor, the figures might have sounded compelling. But Gary and I knew the game might be quickly coming to a close. Extracta didn't seem to be the kind of company to walk away without a fight, so we thought there might be a still larger bid to come from them.

As we dissected the latest offer, my Blackberry rang. Don Cunningham, the CEO of Fletcher-Broussard, had come to New York on business and wanted to get together. Gary and I found this both exciting and curious. Exciting because he hadn't forgotten us and might be looking to jump into the Red Metal cage match. Curious because CEOs usually kept their personal distance from us, not wanting to spark any collusion or conspiracy rumors.

I invited Don to the Penn Club, a gathering place for University of Pennsylvania graduates, including me and my Wharton buddies. We had dinner in the Presidents and Provosts Room. I figured with all the mahogany, Don would feel as if he were sitting in his executive dining room back in Alabama. Plus, it afforded far more privacy than a place like the Algonquin, just a stone's throw away.

I arrived ten minutes before Don to get us situated in a far corner so we could speak privately. He walked in with the slow gait of a road warrior who'd spent one too many hours in meetings and needed to relax. His arms stayed nearly motionless at his sides as the waiter escorted him to our table. His shoulders slouched as if he had run out of energy. The wrinkled pants of his navy-blue suit indicated he'd been on the road a few days too long.

Don joined me in a Glenlivet on the rocks, and then another. He had come to New York to visit with some of Fletcher-Broussard's major investors. Most of them, however, wanted to talk about the shit storm revolving around Red Metal.

Everywhere he went, people wanted to talk about Gary and me, and Galileo Capital. We had impressed people by shaking up an old-line firm like Red Metal. Mainly, Don's shareholders enjoyed seeing Fowler on the ropes.

"I'm a little pissed off at you, though," Don said. "A couple of shareholders asked me whether Fletcher-Broussard might end up buying Red Metal. I'm wondering who put such an idea in their heads, and the only culprit I can think of is sitting across the table from me right now."

Just then the waiter came for our order. Don asked for the ribeye, medium rare, with a baked potato and all the trimmings. I went with the skate stuffed with salmon in a lemon butter sauce. We both asked for more Glenlivet.

"Don, are you suggesting we're spreading rumors to put you in a corner? We're not. I hinted to Red Metal's IR guy that I met with you and Jerry Jack. But I only wanted to get under Fowler's skin. Which we both enjoy doing, right?"

Don smiled and conceded my point. Still, he said, he wouldn't be too quick to give me a pass on rumors starting to circulate around Fletcher-Broussard. He disliked the rumors, he said, because they made his stock price jump around without reason. That seemed lame to me. Rumors swirl around companies every day. They might push the stock price up or down a little, but over time, the rumors either prove to be true or they don't. If they don't, their effect on stock price disappears. If they do, their effect gets factored in, and the stock price rises or falls according to the market's reaction. But for whatever reason, the rumors bothered Don.

I proposed a more obvious reason for the rumors.

"I'm guessing some of your savvier shareholders, those who know the copper business well, think acquiring Red Metal would be a logical move for you, and a good one. Their sentiments may have nothing to do with rumors but rather with their conclusion that acquiring Red Metal would make sense for Fletcher-Broussard. After all, I think you and Jerry Jack have a much better understanding of the business than Fowler does. You never saddled yourselves with bullshit copper collars that reduced your profits, right? Shareholders see the moves he's made, and they think the company could be run better by another management team. Like you and Jerry Jack."

As I expected, a little flattery went a long way with Don.

"Maybe you're right. I'll admit I asked several times where these rumors came from, and people said they hadn't heard any rumors. Maybe I'm just learning the reaction to our acquiring Red Metal would be positive."

"It sure would be from this shareholder!" I said.

"Yeah, well, you'd be happy if Boeing or Purina or Wells Fargo acquired Red Metal, as long as the price suited you. True?"

Now I conceded his point. Still, I reiterated Fletcher-Broussard and Red Metal would be a natural fit for one another. F-B would be a bigger, stronger player in the world's copper markets, and its future would be assured for decades to come.

"Could be," Don said. "Could be. I guess we'll both just have to keep an eye on what happens north of the border."

EIGHTEEN

All was not quiet on the Canadian front. You'll recall in the poker game to win Eagle Crest, Extracta had turned up the heat by raising its all-cash bid from $47.25 a share to $53.10. Red Metal countered with an offer of $72.63 for NICAN, which in turn would result in an offer to Eagle Crest shareholders of $57.10 a share with a cash component of $26.73.

About a week later, Extracta announced a new, all-cash offer of $56.25 a share for Eagle Crest. It surprised no one—certainly not Gary and me—that Extracta's offer gained momentum. Again, we saw those all-important words—"all cash."

The Eagle Crest board members soldiered on for a while, saying they endorsed the Red Metal NICAN offer as the best long-term deal. Eagle Crest's major shareholders, however, quickly signaled they preferred Extracta's deal, and by early August, the Eagle Crest board backed the Extracta offer. It reminded me of the old saying: "Show me where the people are going, for I must follow, for I am their leader." Not long after, Eagle Crest belonged to Extracta.

Fowler, during his June news conference in Toronto, had said Red Metal would pursue NICAN regardless of whether it succeeded in acquiring Eagle Crest. It made little sense to Gary and me. Without Eagle Crest, Fowler lost the ability to achieve significant savings. True to his word, however, he continued to press ahead in pursuit of NICAN.

Before Red Metal stepped foot in Canada, you'll recall, another Canadian company, Hecht Komando, announced a bid to acquire NICAN. Investors had largely ignored the Hecht bid once Red Metal did its grandstanding in Toronto. Hecht Komando's CEO, however, refused to be ignored.

Bill Brighton stood out as a hybrid in the mining industry, according to the Hecht website. He had operations credentials, holding a degree in mining engineering and coming up through the iron and uranium industries. He had worked as a foreman, but he saw he needed a different kind of education to reach the top of his industry. He headed to Dartmouth for his MBA, which put him on the fast track in Canadian mining.

A simple force drove his business objectives, he once told the Vancouver Mercury: "Hecht Komando faces the same challenge all mining companies face. Our assets are shrinking every day. Any mining company worth its salt is trying to acquire three to five large ore bodies. It's the only way to sustain the company for shareholders in the next generation." And that, obviously, is why he wanted NICAN. Well, that, and the ego thrill of bagging one of Canada's premier mining companies.

The hostile bid he and Hecht Komando had on the table, various news reports indicated, came after Brighton had tried to engineer a friendly merger to bring together Hecht Komando, NICAN and Eagle Crest. Supposedly, NICAN spurned the offer because NICAN executives believed Hecht's metallurgical coal and zinc reserves didn't fit logically with its nickel business; China had plenty of zinc and coal, but not enough copper and nickel, so a Red Metal/NICAN/Eagle

Crest merger, the NICAN board reasoned, seemed ideal. Once NICAN showed Brighton the door, he decided to try to push his way back in with a hostile bid.

The bid came in May 2006, a month and a half before Red Metal's. Once Red Metal acted, Hecht Komando never withdrew its offer, but the offer never gained traction because it fell nearly 20 percent below the Red Metal offer made in late June.

I can only guess Brighton and his financial wizards stewed night and day for about a month. Then, in late July, Hecht Komando announced a new offer of $74.25 in stock and cash. The offer came in below Red Metal's proposal of approximately $77.40, but (you'll see a common theme here) it contained a great deal more cash than Red Metal's offer. (The value of Red Metal's stock-and-cash offer for NICAN had grown because its stock price rose after Extracta won the poker game for Eagle Crest.) Early reports said NICAN shareholders wanted to hear more.

NICAN, of course, reiterated its commitment to the Red Metal offer. NICAN executives helped put together the Red Metal NICAN deal, so they had pride of authorship. The top brass at NICAN would get to keep their jobs, and stay in Toronto, if the Red Metal deal went through. And the $475 million breakup fee pledged to Red Metal if the deal fell through wouldn't have to be paid.

NICAN shareholders, I'm sure, enjoyed being part of their own version of Let's Make a Deal. And just as they weighed a choice between Door No. 1 and Door No. 2, a new game master came down the aisle with an offer to take Door No. 3.

Soon after the turn of the millennium, the world started noticing the increasing power of developing nations. Since the mid-1970s, the G7 countries—Canada, France, Germany, Italy, Japan, the United Kingdom and the United States—began meeting several times a year to discuss such issues as global economic governance, international security, and energy policy. Between 1998 and 2014, Russia had a seat at the table, and the group came to be known as the G8 countries. But after Russia annexed Crimea in 2014, the G7 gang tossed Russia from the group.

The G7 countries account for about two thirds of the world's net global wealth, 45 percent of global domestic product and 30 percent of global purchasing power. They represent the "haves" in a world of "haves" and "have nots." In a game of Monopoly, they own Park Place, the railroads, the utilities, and anything else worth having.

But in 2001, Goldman Sachs turned the spotlight on four nations with the potential to move alongside the G7 countries as superstars. By 2050, Goldman Sachs said, the combined economies of the BRIC nations—Brazil, Russia, India and China—could eclipse the combined economies of the G7 countries.

As if to prove the point, in mid-August 2006, Brazil's Amazonia Mines made a hostile bid for NICAN. Amazonia came on the scene in the early 1940s. Originally, the Brazilian government owned about 80 percent of the company, and even today, it holds a substantial interest. As is the case in most developing nations, Amazonia lacked management expertise during the company's early days. Over the years, however, Amazonia found its footing, and by 1990, it ranked at No. 294 on the Fortune 500 list of the world's largest companies. It grew exponentially once it started developing the huge iron reserves discovered in the Amazon in the 1960s.

Amazonia wanted to flex its muscles outside Brazil. It already had moved into other parts of South America and Africa, and it eagerly looked to the day it would have holdings in North America. NICAN provided a perfect target for the company's ambitions. In early August, it made its intentions clear with an all-cash bid for NICAN of $77.40 a share, or $17.5 billion.

Amazonia's announcement set off a flurry of media coverage and media speculation. Would Red Metal make a new offer? Would it change the structure of its bid to increase the cash component? Did Red Metal management have the fortitude to stay at the table? Would Red Metal's investors tolerate an increased bid for NICAN?

For its part, Red Metal retreated to the standard response of most publicly traded companies when things get ugly: "As a matter of corporate policy, Red Metal does not comment on rumor or speculation in the market." Which often is a way of saying, "Oh, shit! We have no idea what we're going to do. When we figure it out, we may or may not tell you. Now, go away."

As Red Metal's largest investor, I gladly commented when Bloomberg's Jim Stevenson called.

"I'm not in position to evaluate whether an Amazonia-NICAN merger makes sense. I don't know enough about Amazonia. I can tell you this, however: We have opposed Red Metal's Canadian schemes since their announcement in June. We laughed at the idea of taking on enormous debt to effect the Red Metal-NICAN-Eagle Crest merger. Now, since Eagle Crest fell out of the picture, bringing together Red Metal and NICAN makes absolutely no sense.

"The increased debt will drag Red Metal down, and the touted savings virtually disappear because most of them would have resulted from bringing NICAN and Eagle Crest together. I, for one, will be glad when the Red Metal-NICAN deal falls apart. I'm sure many investors agree."

Jim asked me whether Galileo had pursued obtaining the services of a proxy solicitor to encourage shareholders to vote against Red Metal. Gary and I had explored this several times but had taken a more direct approach. We worked through the public records to find the handful of shareholders who controlled most of the stock, and we gave them a call.

"We considered going with a proxy solicitor, Jim. But after discussions with shareholders heavily invested in Red Metal, we see no reason to spend our money. There is little support out there for a Red Metal-NICAN combination, almost none, I'd say. Mark my words: This deal is dead on arrival."

In mid-August, Red Metal kept the game going. It made no further effort to increase its bid for NICAN, but it announced a shareholder vote for Sept. 25 on its proposal to acquire the company. Then it went on radio silence. The name of Todd Williamson, Red Metal's IR guy, appeared regularly in the media over the next few weeks, but it always came with some version of the words, "No comment."

The day after Red Metal's announcement, NICAN's CEO, Steve Berkman, said NICAN still supported the Red Metal cash-and-stock offer but acknowledged the Amazonia bid could provide a superior result for shareholders. For that reason, NICAN would engage in discussions with Amazonia's senior management.

A Canadian stock market analyst, Ken Morgan of Redmont Capital, told the Toronto World Red Metal's offer now stood as the weakest on the table.

"The NICAN board can't walk away from the Red Metal offer because they have agreements in place," he said. "But they're obligated to get the best deal possible for their shareholders, so they have to talk to Amazonia, and they have to present all offers to their shareholders. My guess is Hecht Komando will leave the bidding war, NICAN shareholders will vote for the Amazonia offer, NICAN will pay Red Metal a hefty breakup fee, and Canada will make room for two major foreign mining companies, Switzerland's Extracta and Brazil's Amazonia."

Morgan got it almost all right. He missed only one thing. Three weeks later, Red Metal withdrew its offer for NICAN and canceled its shareholder vote.

Berkman said NICAN's proxy solicitation indicated its shareholders would not support the Red Metal offer. Fowler said NICAN would have been an attractive acquisition at the price it offered but acknowledged projected savings from the merger declined significantly after Eagle Crest came off the table.

I told you up front I wanted to move on Red Metal because its management hadn't figured out how quickly their world had been changing. Initially, I saw they had no feel for how long and how strong the demand for copper would be, and how the price of copper would stay elevated. That made Red Metal a sitting duck for a hedge-fund manager.

I came to see Red Metal had missed something even bigger. A great divide had developed between mining companies with a 20th-century worldview and those smoothly making the transition into the 21st century. Those stuck in the 20th century—Red Metal and NICAN, for example—placed a high value on geologists and engineers, and they followed the slow-moving, established pattern of exploring hunches until they found one resulting in a viable mine that could take years to open. Those who moved into the 21st century put swashbuckling financiers and bankers in their CEO chairs. They knew how to assemble capital quickly to lock down already developed acquisitions and grow fast.

Fowler once told me timeframes in the mining business are glacial. He embodied the perspective of a 20th-century executive who had learned to take his time building and developing mines. The new breed pursued rapid growth. They found good assets and good fits with their businesses, and when they did, they quickly pulled the money together— cold, hard cash—to buy what they wanted. In place of glaciers, they substituted floods of cash. They awakened and energized a once sleepy industry, and they left people like Jeff Fowler drowning in their wake.

With the NICAN-Eagle Crest deal, Fowler tried to play the game, but as a rookie among seasoned veterans, he didn't stand a chance. The game had changed, and his skills, though impressive, could not carry him to victory.

NINETEEN

Funny thing. Once Red Metal called off its vote on the NICAN deal, I found myself feeling more charitable toward Jeff Fowler. Maybe it's my Catholic training. In our soccer games back at Fenwick High, we learned to pursue victory with a vengeance. After the game, though, the priests always made us shake hands with the other team, whether we won or lost. Eventually, I learned opponents aren't necessarily enemies. The game is one thing, and winning is great, but being a mensch is more important than either. Or that's what the priests told us. I began feeling menschly toward Fowler.

Of course, circumstances and economics still had us inextricably bound together. I owned 10 percent of his company, after all. And I felt more sanguine. Once the NICAN deal fell through, Red Metal's stock price started moving up again. Good news, but I thought significantly higher gains could be achieved. I'd continue to try to get those gains, probably through getting Red Metal sold to another company.

But for the next couple of months, Fowler laid low, and I did too. Red Metal made little news during that time. Other than announcing a contribution of $1 million to support Hispanic/Latino learning initiatives at Arizona State University, it stayed below the radar.

Frankly, Gary and I needed a break. All throughout the summer, the Red Metal NICAN deal absorbed us. Reporters didn't often call us to comment, and we couldn't do much but watch events unfold. But we became obsessed with every news story and every piece of data we could get, and we watched our pot of money rise or fall every day depending on market rumors and investor reaction. We found it almost as exhausting as being a diehard Chicago Cubs fan, our other summer passion, and it hadn't gone well. The Cubs ended up 30 games under .500 in 2006, in the cellar of the National League Central Division.

Events drained us, and in late September, we asked Shannon and Jessica where they'd like to go for a minivacation. To our surprise, they both said Arizona.

"Do you know how hot it is in Arizona, still? Even in September? It's not like New York. Temperatures don't break after Labor Day. It can be hot as hell there till the end of October," Gary said.

Jessica dug in. "You're thinking of Phoenix. This time, we want to go north. It's cool up there. Let's fly into Flagstaff. There's lots to see. I've been reading about it. The Grand Canyon, the Painted Desert, the Petrified Forest—lots of stuff. We can even stand on the corner in Winslow, just like the song."

Shannon had an interesting thought. "Why don't you see if you can get your buddy Mike the limo driver to show us around? He'd probably welcome a chance to get out of Phoenix this time of year, and I'll bet he knows northern Arizona like a native. Tell him he can bring his wife, mistress or whatever other lover he might have. It'd be a chance to do a good thing for a good guy."

And so, a week later, Mike and his girlfriend, Karina, picked us up at the Flagstaff airport. She was a dark-haired, dark-eyed beauty, probably 10 years younger than Mike and, like him and the Kardashians, Armenian. Think of Karina as a more beautiful Kardashian sister. Gary and I definitely did everything we could think of to make her feel welcome! Lots of small talk, lots of friendly questions, lots of going out of our way to find ways to be near her. Shannon and Jessica showed more amusement than jealousy while watching us. And really, they had nothing to worry about. We loved them to death, and we had no appetite for going through a third divorce, but we're not above reverting to horny school boys in the presence of a beautiful woman.

Before we flew out, Mike told us we should stay at the La Posada in Winslow, which lies about an hour east of Flagstaff on I-40. He made all the arrangements, and he greeted us when we landed. As we got off the Netjets flight, mountain-fresh air and a temperature of about 70 welcomed us to Arizona. Jessica and Shannon proved to be right. This would be a great spot to unwind for a few days.

As soon as we hit the highway, we obviously had come to a world totally different from the one we had seen two hours south in Phoenix. At 7,000 feet, we found ourselves in high country. Saguaro cactuses and palm trees dotted the flat-as-a-pancake Phoenix landscape. (Phoenix had a few "mountains," but I'd call them "mountainettes." Nothing more than about 3,000 feet tall. Phoenix rests among them in what it calls the Valley of the Sun.) Up around Flagstaff, majestic Ponderosa pines soar and point to the San Francisco Peaks, which reach almost 13,000 feet.

"When we moved to Phoenix from Niagara Falls, my parents sold their skiing equipment," Mike said. "They didn't have a clue they could drive two hours north for some really challenging slopes. They bought new equipment and brought my sisters and me up here often in the winter. If you like to ski, come back sometime when it's cold."

Mike had stocked a full bar for us in his limo, so we had a mellow ride over to Winslow. When we pulled into town, we saw Winslownians had done all they could to take advantage of the free plug the Eagles gave them in 1972 with their first hit, *Take It Easy*.

The "Standin' on the Corner" Park is more like a small monument to the song, complete with a bronze statue of a balladeer resting his guitar upright on one foot while he holds the headstock in his right hand. His left thumb is looped into his jeans pocket. He's leaning against an old-fashioned lamppost topped by an onion-shaped globe with an incandescent bulb inside. Above his head is the police-badge-shaped Route 66 marker, only it contains the words "Standin' on the Corner." There's a mural behind him of "a girl, my Lord, in a flatbed Ford" taking a look at him. Thanks to Mike's limo bar, we had become laid-back tourists, so we took advantage of the photo op. Mike took the photo while the five of us gathered around the lamppost. Gary and I tried our best not to ogle Karina, but one look at the photo would tell you we failed.

The whole town couldn't have had more than about 10,000 people, so despite Mike's best intentions, I didn't expect much from the La Posada Hotel. Was I ever wrong!

You've heard of the Harvey Girls, right? They're named after Fred Harvey, the restaurateur and entrepreneur who created the first restaurant chain in the United States. He especially loved the Southwest, and he made it his mission to civilize the area by introducing linen, silverware, china, crystal and the grace of the Harvey Girls throughout the area. Harvey developed and ran all the hotels and restaurants along the Santa Fe Railway, including La Posada, which means "The Inn" in Spanish.

He hired Mary Colter as the architect for La Posada. She's known for her Phantom Ranch buildings at the Grand Canyon, but she considered the Spanish Colonial Revival, hacienda-style La Posada her masterpiece. She had full control of everything from the design of the buildings to the clothing worn by the maids. Over the years, La Posada has played host to everyone from Shirley Temple to John Wayne to Jimmy Cagney to Diane Keaton and the Crown Prince of Japan.

Mike made sure to get deluxe rooms for all of us. For about $130 a night, we had giant rooms with whirlpool baths. We would have dropped $1,700 or more a night in New York for the same accommodations.

We had dinner our first night in the hotel's Turquoise Room. The women opted for chicken breasts. Mike told Gary and me to order the Wild Wild Platter, with samples of quail, elk, bison and wild boar. Not something I'd normally choose, but I savored every bite! Mike went with the Churro Lamb Sampler.

Eventually, talk turned to Red Metal.

Mike said he had driven several executives to and from Red Metal lately, and he'd also been talking to his friends who work there.

"I'm hearing the headquarters office is like a morgue. Not much work going on, and apparently, no one much cares. People spend time in front of their computers looking busy, but they're doing everything from online crossword puzzles to checking out recipes.

"People who don't work in cubes have glass-fronted offices, so it's easy to see what they're doing. I've been told even Fowler spends an unusual amount of time just reading the Wall Street Journal or sitting with his nose buried in a book. He seems to have taken a fancy to John Grisham's novels.

"Work is getting done at the mines. You still have to get the copper out of the ground. But at headquarters, people seem to be mostly treading water. One guy told me he used to have two or three meetings a day, but now it's more like one a week."

I wasn't surprised. I figured everyone in corporate worked marathon hours during the summer of Red Metal NICAN. It wouldn't be unusual for people to crash for a while once the market scotched the deal.

"So, Mike, who have you been picking up for Red Metal? Anyone interesting?"

"I don't know who most of them are, at least not by name. A lot of them are managers from their mines around the world. They'll do anything to get back to civilization for a few days. You New Yorkers might not think of Phoenix as civilized, but I imagine if you spent some time living at a mine site in Africa, you might sing a different tune."

I told him actually, Phoenix really impressed us, and we thought we'd be coming back from time to time. We had plenty left to explore. We liked the food, and we liked the vibe of the place. Mike said he liked the tips we'd be bringing him.

"There's been one of set of guys I can't figure out," he said. "They fly into Cutter too, just like you did and just like Fowler does. They have a big Gulfstream, and they seem well-lubricated when they get into the limo. They're like a throwback to the '50s in a lot of ways. Good southern gentlemen, but there's something about them that makes me think I wouldn't want to buy a used car from either one. They kind of remind me of Foghorn P. Leghorn in the old Warner Brothers cartoons. You know: 'Ah say, boy, ah say...'" They tip well. Not like you, but they tip well. I've picked them up a couple of times lately."

I asked Mike whether he could come up with names for either of them.

"Did you ever watch Happy Days? Ron Howard played Richie Cunningham. I can't remember the guy's first name, but I know his last name was Cunningham. I remember because I associated him with Richie."

"Don," I said. "The guy's first name was Don, right?"

"Yeah, that's it. Do you know him?"

"I've met him a couple of times. He seems like a good guy."

That's all I volunteered for Mike, but again, he gave me more than my money's worth, and I liked what I heard.

For the next few days, we made day trips on I-40, taking in all the sights Jessica mentioned before we made the trip. We were two hours behind Birmingham, so I could easily try to reach Don Cunningham after our morning breakfasts. Each time, though, Sherri told me Mr. Cunningham was unavailable to take my call. I saw it as a good sign.

After five days, Mike and Karina dropped us at the Flagstaff airport, and I paid him $5,000. Not a bad haul for a few days of an all-expenses-paid vacation and a chance to share a luxurious bed with Karina. Pretty impressive that a limo driver could land a woman like her! But then, he could be quite the charmer.

We headed back to Teterboro. All four of us felt relaxed and recharged. Gary and I slept like babies almost all the way home.

TWENTY

A couple of weeks after we returned to New York, Red Metal issued its third-quarter earnings release. Gary and I dialed in to the investor conference call but kept quiet. Analysts who asked questions sounded like hospital visitors to a terminally ill patient—respectful, and well aware something drastic could be imminent.

Third-quarter net income came in at $888 million, or $4.36 a share. That included the first of the breakup payments from NICAN—$125 million—and another $350 million would be coming in shortly.

Most of the questions, of course, revolved around what Red Metal planned to do with the $4.1 billion in cash that had accumulated over the past couple of years. Fowler's answer, sadly, stuck to the same talking points I'd heard ever since I started studying the company.

"The cash situation being what it is, we need to do something sooner rather than later," he acknowledged. Then he reiterated variations on three of the four points I had first heard a year and a half earlier—invest in existing businesses, improve the quality of Red Metal's asset base (with a possible acquisition), and reward shareholders. Only one point had fallen off the list: strengthen the balance sheet. With all that cash, the balance sheet looked more bloated than ever, and the whole world knew it.

Shortly after the call, my Blackberry rang. Jim Stevenson from Bloomberg wanted a comment.

"Mr. Fowler had it right," I said. "That stockpile of cash he's sitting on is begging to be used productively or returned to shareholders. But as far as I'm concerned, he and his team had their chance, and it's time for them to move offstage. I'm guessing market realities will take them out soon, and somebody stronger will take their place."

Jim asked me whether Galileo had made good on its threat to find somebody to buy Red Metal. I told him I couldn't be specific, but we had been talking with possible buyers. We believed something dramatic would happen soon.

Most of the day, I reviewed the coverage coming through on our Bloomberg terminal. A headline from a Tucson newspaper took me aback: Red Metal Reports $4 Billion Windfall. It made no sense. The story correctly reported third-quarter net income of $888 million and said the company's cash balance now stood at $4.1 billion. Obviously, the $4.1 billion in cash couldn't be called a "windfall." It had built up over time. I'll never get over how ignorant many business reporters are of basic knowledge, like the difference between income statements and balance sheets.

After the earnings call, Red Metal faded back into the woodwork. I tried periodically to communicate with Don Cunningham at Fletcher-Broussard, but I could not reach him. Sherri, my friend at the reception desk in Birmingham, continued to refuse to put me through and wouldn't tell me where he might be.

• • •

Shannon used the lull in Red Metal action to get me more involved with setting up the Brown Family Foundation. The more she drew me in, the more intrigued I became.

As she explained it, we could expand our reach and influence—and our social circle—by using our foundation strategically. Her passion revolved around preventing women's health complications during pregnancy and childbirth. Mine, she had assessed correctly, centered on architecture.

"So think about this, Dave. With the money in the foundation, we can fund projects to bring us together with leaders in their fields. We can get first looks at cutting-edge research in healthy pregnancies. We can have access to the world's greatest contemporary architects. We can help pay for the education of the next generation of leaders in women's medicine and architecture. To me, it would be a lot more exciting than rolling Jeff Fowler for as many millions as you can get out of him. Be honest. Would you rather have a good meal and an evening of conversation with Jeff Fowler or Jeanne Gang? If we use this foundation correctly, you and Jeanne and I could become the best of friends."

I had to laugh at being fingered for "rolling" Fowler. I liked to characterize what I did as creating excellent returns for the people who trusted me with their money. But yeah, I had to admit, things became personal sometimes, and despite my recent, more menschly sentiments, I'd gotten a charge or two out of watching Fowler squirm. And maybe it would not stand as my finest moment.

Clearly Shannon had been doing her research. I knew about Jeanne Gang, but she wouldn't have been known to Shannon unless Shannon had been reading up on architecture. Chicago architecture.

Gang had received a contract earlier in 2006 for Aqua, an 82-story residential tower on Lake Michigan and the largest project ever awarded to an American firm headed by a woman.

I'd seen the drawings online. Gang imagined, by using curving concrete balconies of different widths, floor by floor, she could produce the illusion of the Chicago wind creating ripples on water or fabric. During my lifetime, I'd never seen such an exciting proposal for a Chicago building. Of course I'd like to have dinner with Jeanne Gang!

Even though the foundation money came from us, Shannon said, we'd be smart to establish an advisory board to help us select projects to fund. A board could serve as a buffer between us and all the people who would want to hit us up for money. It could help us think through the guidelines for projects we would and wouldn't fund. And, she reiterated, we could expand our social circle to include people who would fascinate us.

I had to admit, for a kid who grew up in Oak Park, the son of a meat cutter, I started to find this whole foundation thing attractive. And I knew Shannon could make it happen. Her charm and her command of the social graces far exceeded mine, and she'd be able to get an audience with virtually anyone she wished. I smiled as I saw how much pleasure she would get from the Brown Family Foundation. The $10 million in seed money suddenly didn't seem difficult to part with.

Within a week, she had set up a dinner in San Francisco with RK Stewart, the incoming president of the American Institute of Architects. He suggested we stay at the Ritz-Carlton at Half Moon Bay, which looked like an Old World, five-story castle sitting on a bluff overlooking the Pacific Ocean. It was, of course, ritzy, with magnificent furnishings, perfectly manicured lawns and golf courses, and breathtaking views of the bay. RK joined us for dinner there.

It surprised me to learn that, like me, RK originally came from the Midwest, having grown up in St. Louis. I suspected he rooted for the baseball Cardinals (it's almost a given if you're from St. Louis), so I congratulated him on the team's recent World Series victory over Detroit. He offered his condolences for my lifelong obsession with the Cubs.

"I owe my passion for architecture to trips to Chicago," he said. "My grandfather was an executive with the Cotton Belt Railroad, and he'd often take me on train trips to Chicago. When I saw those glorious buildings downtown, I knew what I wanted to do with my life."

RK and I also shared a love for Frank Lloyd Wright's work. He'd been to Oak Park many times. It delighted me to learn he had developed the master plan for renovating Wright's Marin County Civic Center.

RK said the next century would be revolutionary in architecture. He told Shannon and me about Architecture 2030, an ambitious initiative to make new and renovated buildings carbon neutral by 2030.

"Over the next 20 years, an area equal to three and a half times the entire built environment of the U.S. will be redesigned, reshaped and rebuilt worldwide. If we don't make these buildings carbon neutral, there's no way we'll beat the problem of climate change. There's a lot architects can do—anything from orienting the building correctly to using passive heating and cooling to incorporating fossil-fuel-free energy.

"A building's aesthetics are important, of course, and I think beautiful design is what intrigues both of us about architecture. But the real challenge will be to make buildings both beautiful and environmentally sound. Folks like you can help make it happen with research grants, prize money, scholarships and other initiatives."

We talked late into the night about the future of architecture. Shannon made a smart move in arranging this meeting as the first of our exploratory discussions. She had hooked me forever on the idea of doing significant work through the Brown Family Foundation. She also coaxed RK into agreeing to be a member of the advisory board.

The next week, Shannon had us in Atlanta for a meeting with Helene Gayle, the CEO of CARE USA. Dr. Gayle told us CARE saw maternal mortality as a top priority in the fight against poverty. In some countries, she said, one in seven women dies during pregnancy or childbirth. Tremendous progress had been and will be made, so if we chose to focus on maternal mortality, our support could make a real, lasting difference.

She and Shannon hit it off immediately. Dr. Gayle probably wouldn't be a candidate for our advisory board because her organization could benefit directly from our work. But she would happily put us in touch with good candidates.

By the time we returned to New York, I shared Shannon's dreams for the Brown Family Foundation. We could work on it together, and it could really achieve some good things for the world. The world!

Suddenly, I thought back to my trip with the Catholic school teachers on the Staten Island Ferry, the ones who had wanted to do something "worthwhile" with their lives. Was I becoming like them? No, I'd never be like them, I thought. I have so much more, and I've done so much more. I have a sophistication they'll never have. Like the rich young man in the New Testament, I imagine I would balk if Jesus told me to follow him by selling all I have and giving to the poor to have treasure in heaven. (Besides, I've never heard him talk to me directly.)

But maybe Shannon had it right. Maybe I had better things to do in life than roll Jeff Fowler and his kind for as much as I could.

TWENTY-ONE

The big announcement came the Monday before Thanksgiving. Fletcher-Broussard would acquire Red Metal for $25.9 billion, or $126.46 a share. When I'd gone to bed the previous Friday, the stock had closed at $95.02, so Jerry Jack and Don committed to shelling out a 33 percent premium for the company.

Fletcher-Broussard stacked up as the smaller company, with a market cap of about $11.3 billion to Red Metal's $19.4 billion. To make it happen, Fletcher-Broussard went about $17.5 billion into debt. Shortly after the deal closed, it raised about $5.6 billion by issuing new stock. Normally, this would have lowered the price per share because of dilution. The market, however, believed copper prices would only increase, and the stock price never took a hit. Fletcher-Broussard used the money raised from the stock issuance, and the money it made hand over fist from selling high-priced copper, to pay down a good chunk of the debt within a year.

Gary and I had been proved right. Red Metal could have been a much more aggressive borrower than it had been, if it had pursued the right, all-cash deal. Earlier, we would gladly have supported an acquisition of Fletcher-Broussard by Red Metal. It couldn't happen now, however, because Red Metal had lost all credibility with investors.

Jeff Fowler told the media he would be retiring. I kept track of him out of curiosity, and he quickly joined the boards of several publicly traded companies. It seemed to be a good path for him, and I heard from a friend of mine at National Airlines that he proved to be one of their most valuable board members. "Brilliantly analytical, in a good way," my friend said. "He's always one of the last to get on board with a change in the company, but by the time he thinks through an issue, there are no surprises. None."

Galileo Capital owned about 10 percent of Red Metal, so we had about $2.6 billion gross coming our way. We'd paid out about $1.3 billion to buy our stock, so we'd made about that much on the deal before taxes. Cut that to about $700 million after taxes, and we still did extraordinarily well. Galileo's share for managing the deal for our investors was 20 percent, or $140 million. Gary and I each walked away with a figure north of $60 million, and our employees did well too.

As you can imagine, our holidays rocked! I told Beth, my admin, I would make myself scarce for about a month. She knew how to reach me, but I didn't want to hear from anyone unless death came knocking at the door.

Shannon and I decided to celebrate big. National Geographic offers a one-month, around-the-world tour on a specially modified Boeing 757. Two last-minute cancellations let us join the tour starting the day after Christmas. Actually, National Geographic calls it an expedition. "Tour" is just not good enough for this experience.

The plane is configured for 77 passengers instead of the usual 233, so there's lots of room, and you're traveling with the elite of the world. (Most of your fellow tourists are beyond old, but still, they are elite.) The plane is staffed with three pilots, a chef, a catering officer, eight flight attendants, two engineers, a doctor, and a designated luggage handler.

National Geographic arranges the itinerary so you're almost always traveling west and never cross more than two time zones on any leg of the trip, except for the flight home from Morocco. Jet lag is minimal.

Each hotel and resort is better than the last for luxury, comfort and cuisine. The Raffles Grand Hotel in Angkor, Cambodia, with its 15 acres of formal gardens, turned out to be our favorite. The trip started and ended in Washington, D.C. We, of course, rose to the challenge of making love at every stop in South America, Samoa, Australia, Asia, India, Africa, and the Middle East.

The trip set us back about $60,000 apiece. Today it's more like $80,000. Not much to us either way, and the memories will last a lifetime. Hell, they'll last beyond a lifetime.

We enjoyed it so much that later, we sent my mom and a friend of hers on the same trip. Shannon's idea, not mine. As I said, she's always been better at charm and the social graces.

• • •

In early February 2007, I picked up the phone. The voice on the other end of the line said simply, "I hear you've been trying to reach me."

Don Cunningham wanted to know what I thought of the deal he and Jerry Jack had cut.

"Brilliant," I said, "and highly lucrative for Galileo and me! I'm glad someone in your industry had the vision to see copper could have a prosperous run long enough to make doing a deal like this worthwhile."

Don said the deal would probably close in March and wanted to know whether Galileo would stay invested in Fletcher-Broussard. He knew we'd sold most of our stock—"can't blame you for banking your gains," he said—but he also knew we kept a small portion. We liked management's style, so I assured him we planned to be invested as long as the company's results stayed in line with our investment objectives.

"So you won't be bailing or badmouthing us in the media?"

"Don, you've done extraordinarily well by us. We're planning to stay with you, and if we sell, it won't be because of dissatisfaction with management. It will simply be because we see a better opportunity on the horizon. It's impossible for me to imagine any reason for us not to support you going forward."

Don said Jerry Jack would be staying in Birmingham but he'd be buying a home in Phoenix. He invited me to come by when I ventured into the neighborhood.

● ● ●

I spent the spring and summer of 2007 managing Galileo with Gary. Times were still good, but the bull market started to wear out. It hit its peak on Oct. 11, 2007. I'm sure I don't need to tell you about the setbacks in 2008 and beyond.

In August 2007, out of the blue, I received a call from Todd Williamson, Red Metal's vice president of investor relations. Fletcher-Broussard had its own IR staff, of course. Todd was kept on for a few months so he could be brain-drained, but in July, the company showed him the door. He wanted to come by to discuss possible next steps in his career.

I thought it odd that he'd want to talk with me, but I had a light schedule, and I wanted to hear some of the inside story of Red Metal's last days, so I agreed.

The day Todd came to the office, I returned late from lunch, so Gary treated him to a few rounds on his *Ghostbusters* pinball machine. Turned out Todd had good hands with the flippers, so when I showed up, I had to spend some time watching him play.

"The dude's wiping me out," Gary said, doing a fake bow to pinball royalty when Todd finished. I asked whether Todd might want Gary to sit in on our visit as well, and he warmed to the idea.

"I need as many people as I can recruit to be looking out for my next gig," Todd said, "so if Gary's willing, I'd love to have him sit in with us."

Gary and I had a few years on Todd. He held a bachelor's in accounting from NYU and an MBA with a concentration in finance from Columbia, so he certainly knew his way around a spreadsheet. He started his career in the accounting department at Caterpillar and migrated over to investor relations after a few years. Red Metal spotted him at a mining industry trade show in Las Vegas and stole him away. He liked the idea of being in an exciting industry at an exciting time, and he and his wife wanted to experience the West, so he signed on.

After Red Metal's New York luncheon fiasco, he said, he believed he'd be fired. The idea for the luncheon came from Vassell and Hunt, and no one asked him to weigh in.

"You know how it is. The outside experts always have higher IQ's than the inside help. I told my boss I saw downsides to the lunch, but he never relayed my thoughts, and of course, nobody remembered my concerns when things turned sour."

Once everyone returned to Phoenix, Todd kept waiting for the three-way meeting with himself, his boss and the head of HR.

"Whenever they dump someone, they make sure there's a witness from HR in the room, just in case it's ever claimed the company's reps made promises that weren't made," he said. "I kept expecting the meeting, but it never happened. Until recently, of course. So while the world took shots at the NICAN deal, I just hid in my office and laid low, like most people at headquarters.

"All of us at corporate saw the deal floundering, and the water-cooler talk had it that the board simply couldn't find the will to restructure our NICAN offer to throw in lots more cash. It surprised no one when we lost out to Amazonia. But the whole place went into mass depression. The day we heard about the Fletcher-Broussard deal, we at least had some resolution about the future. And those of us who owned stock had a really good day!

"All during the summer, I kept getting calls from investors, but my boss told me to say nothing except to refer people to the SEC filings. Not very helpful, I know, but at least I kept drawing a paycheck. If I thought someone important enough to get a real response, my boss directed me to refer them to Vassell and Hunt, even though they held a prime spot on Fowler's shit list. As soon as the NICAN deal collapsed, he fired their asses."

Todd said going in, he knew about the track record of IR professionals at Red Metal, so he negotiated to receive 5,000 shares of fully vested stock if he and the company parted ways, for any reason. That and his severance package meant he and his family wouldn't be starving any time soon.

I asked him why, if Fowler had been so mad at him—fairly or not—why hadn't Fowler fired him in a fit of rage? Arizona, like many states in the West, is an "at will" state, which means almost any employee can be terminated at any time for any legal reason or no reason at all, with or without cause.

"Yeah, I wondered myself, so right before Fowler and my boss 'retired' (he used air quotes here), I asked about it. My boss said Fowler knew our little girl had health problems—she has acute lymphoblastic leukemia—so he wanted to avoid heaping another burden on our family right then. You wouldn't guess it, but somewhere beneath that steely front, there's a heart. I'm sure, though, if we hadn't been acquired, Fowler would still be there, and eventually I'd have been just another in a long line of IR guys who had been sent packing."

Todd said an annual holiday lunch marked the last real gathering of Red Metal executives. He attended by virtue of his title and not because of any peace made between him and Fowler.

"We retired the Copper Cup at the lunch. Every year, Red Metal executives would throw $20 in a kitty and place a bet on what copper prices would be one year later. Whoever came closest won the kitty and the right to have his or her name permanently inscribed on the Copper Cup, which the winner prominently displayed in his or her office for a year. Because Red Metal would be no more, the winner at the last lunch would keep the cup, forever.

"Fowler would have loved to walk away with the cup. He as much as said so. But his guess on the price of copper at the end of 2006 came in way low. No surprise there, I guess. And you know, maybe some caution in a CEO is a good thing. You guys might disagree, I guess. Anyway, the guy who won—VP of operations—figured aiming crazy high would be the best way to get the cup. He called it right."

Todd said as an Easterner, raised in Connecticut, he'd now seen more than enough cactus for one lifetime. He wanted to come home and start a new adventure. If Galileo had an open spot, he'd be interested. He admired our gutsiness and thought of us as straight shooters.

Gary and I didn't make any commitments, but we told him we'd keep him in mind and we'd keep an eye out for other opportunities too.

"One more thing I have to ask you, Todd. You remember when the SEC announced an investigation of Galileo? We found out the guy behind the investigation is a close friend of Fowler's. Is there any chance Fowler put him up to it?"

"Absolutely none. I saw almost nothing of Fowler during the summer, what with him spending so much time in Canada. But he had come to the office when the story broke about your being cleared. Fowler interrupted a meeting between my boss and me, carrying a copy of the Wall Street Journal with him. You could feel his disgust. 'Damned moron!' he said.

"My boss and I both flinched, wondering which one of us he meant. It turned out, though, he meant his SEC friend, Clobes. He called the investigation a ham-handed, unsought favor. 'He's a loyal son of a bitch, and we've had a lot of fun together over the years, but God, can he be dumb. Make sure nobody thinks we had anything to do with this.' So no, Fowler didn't put him up to it."

• • •

After he left, Gary and I had a conversation about Todd. I liked the guy, but I didn't think he'd work out for Galileo. Investor relations is a staff function, and people who gravitate to it usually are looking for security, not risk. He came out of NYU and the Columbia business school, and a lot of his skills would be a good fit. But I doubted he'd have the stomach to weather the ups and downs of a hedge fund.

Gary disagreed. He pointed out Todd had the bearing and presentation skills to interact well with our investors. He certainly had the smarts, and just by signing on with Red Metal, he'd shown a willingness to enter a roller-coaster industry. He might actually work out well, if we ever had a need. We could start him at $300,000, give him a huge bonus if things worked out. Ultimately, we could let him buy in as a partner if he liked the hedge-fund life, or let him go if things didn't work out.

We left it at that.

•   •   •

About six weeks after Todd's visit, Gary and I heard from a voice from the past. Fenwick High School's Father Congar called to say he'd booked a flight to New York, and he wanted to take us to lunch. He asked us to meet him to tour the Cloisters and then have lunch together nearby at the New Leaf. He let us know he had left the classroom. Since 2001, he'd been the high school's director of development, so he told us not to be surprised if talk turned to money.

We'd had the occasional run-in with him during our Fenwick days, but the truth is, we thought of him as one of our favorite teachers. Over the years, we had both been pleasantly surprised that, when a major event occurred in the news—in Europe, Asia or Africa—we often had extra insight into it because of his World History class. He'd given us the tools we needed to understand the long history of tensions in the Middle East, the roots of African strife, and the renewed power of Japan and China. We leaned favorably toward helping him out with his fund-raising duties.

Father Congar had chosen wisely. If you want to get the Catholic juices flowing, there's no better place than the Cloisters. It's owned by the Metropolitan Museum of Art, and it sits well north of the city on the Hudson River. It incorporates portions of five different European abbeys. It's filled with statues of Jesus and the saints, medieval altars, illustrated manuscripts and religious tapestries. Gardens have been designed to mimic medieval gardens that might have been found in an abbey. My mind flooded with Gregorian chants. When Gary and I broke away from Father Congar for a restroom break, we admitted feeling swept back to what little piety we had experienced in our lives, which mainly occurred during our years at Fenwick.

The New Leaf kept the vibe alive. The building opened in the 1930s as a gift to the area from John D. Rockefeller. It has a classic, cobblestone exterior, granite archways and oak trusses supporting the dining room's 18-foot ceiling.

At the restaurant, Father Congar offered to pick up the lunch tab, but Gary and I wouldn't hear of it. Lunch was chump change to us, and we thought we'd look cheap if our names showed up on his expense report.

We heard from Fenwick often, of course, through alumni magazines and mailed fund-raising pitches, but no one had ever bothered to come see us. I have to tell you, no matter how cynical you might be about people looking for money, it's flattering to be visited face to face.

"Here's a little something special for both of you from home," he said after we ordered. He handed us each an envelope. Our mothers had placed little notes inside, saying hello and urging us to take good care of Father Congar. A nice touch, I thought. Manipulative, but nice!

After some small talk about Oak Park and bringing each other up to date about our lives, Father Congar started steering the conversation where he wanted it to go.

"At Fenwick, we often talked about the importance of living a life of service," he told us. "Of course, for us priests, we didn't have much choice. We wanted a life of servanthood, and we don't have much perspective on the other side. I would no more know how to make the money you guys have made than I'd know how to get to the moon.

"But still, I may be richer than you in some ways. I can cite centuries of wisdom that serving is what enriches us, not money. Every time you serve someone, even if it's just to hold a door for somebody, you have a chance to see the most important things you offer aren't things at all. Your attention, your time, your presence, those are the things people remember. They touch people. They also help us remember a lot of people have helped us, we benefited from their help, and we can step up and pay it forward to others."

As I looked at him, I thought he really hadn't aged much. His jowls had grown and gotten a bit flabbier. His hair had thinned. Somehow, his demeanor had softened. It might have been because his job required him to be deferential to us, his potential donors. But I didn't think so. Odd as it seemed, I actually thought he had gotten to be, well, saintly.

His words provoked a weird mix of feelings in me. I'd spent my life since college amassing money. I did it well, I enjoyed it, and I saw no need to apologize for it. No one handed me anything.

But I had to admit, early in my career, several people took time to show me how the markets worked. My Wharton professors helped me develop my skills. And my parents, especially my mom, made me the focus of their lives. I'd be nowhere without them. So yeah, Father Congar had a point about other people moving me forward.

Gary didn't reflect much on Father Congar's comments, but our lunch set off a conversation within me that lasted for months. I thought about the simplicity and sincerity of those Catholic teachers on the ferry. I started thinking seriously about what to do with my life, now that paying the bills would never be a worry.

Before we left the New Leaf, Father Congar turned to the specific reason he wanted to see us.

"I hope you'll see this as a chance to do what we've been talking about, to serve," he said. "Fenwick is working on some major improvements and renovations, and we need new soccer fields. We want to do it right—beautiful turf, comfortable bleachers, a modern scoreboard, a great sound system, refreshment stands. It'll take a million and a half. Plus, we want to establish an endowment fund of another $200,000. We'll use the interest to make sure we always have enough money for maintenance and repairs.

"We're hoping you two, together, might make this happen for us. We'll name it for you in perpetuity, of course. The Brown-Gutzler Soccer Complex. You don't have to commit today. I'll leave these plans with you. I'll call you in a couple of weeks, but get in touch with me any time if you have questions."

"Do you know why we called our hedge fund Galileo Capital?" Gary asked him. "It all goes back to a day in World History when you and I had an exchange about Galileo. David and I drew a couple of days of detention together after mouthing off to you. Well, I mouthed off, and he laughed, which is about the same thing, I guess."

Father Congar said he remembered the exchange, all too well.

"The detention made lifelong friends of David and me," Gary said. "We named our hedge fund in honor of you and your bringing us together. I don't do much talking in this partnership, but I think I can speak for David and tell you we'll do it. One thing, though. Let's call it the Galileo Capital Soccer Complex."

I had no objections. Neither did Father Congar.

• • •

During 2007, both before and after Father Congar's visit, Shannon and I engaged in long conversations about what we'd like to do with our lives. She, of course, saw us fully committed to the Brown Family Foundation. I certainly liked the opportunities it presented, but I couldn't get used to the idea of walking away from Galileo. I liked the idea of doing more community service, but when things went right, I loved the adrenalin rush of watching dollars pile up like snow during a tough Chicago winter.

On the other hand, managing a hedge fund often took 80 hours a week, and I found myself enjoying the slower pace that came after a major ordeal like our pursuit of Red Metal. I started to think, even if I left Galileo, I could always get back in the game. Meantime, new adventures called. Eventually, they started looking more attractive than plugging away at a hedge fund.

In November, I had a long talk with Gary, telling him I wanted to shake up my life. He didn't seem overly surprised, but he wouldn't let me just skate off.

He said our investors knew me, not him, as the face of Galileo. If I left too abruptly, without creating a smooth transition, there'd be a rush on the bank, and unlike Jimmy Stewart in It's a Wonderful Life, we wouldn't be able to stop it, and Gary would be out of work. He insisted I come up with a game plan to ensure investors they'd be in good hands once I left.

"I'll help you, Gary, but here's the deal: You're going to have to be more visible too. We can find a front man, but people should know you make up a lot of the brainpower in Galileo. They'll feel better if they know you've been driving much of our strategy all along and you're staying."

Gary wanted to recruit Todd Williamson into Galileo. I had my misgivings, but I figured Gary would have to live with whoever came on, so he should be able to decide. Todd came on board soon after.

For the next few months, the three of us visited with all our major investors. Most of them actually warmed nicely to Todd, and they appreciated learning more about Gary and the pivotal role he played in making Galileo a success. By July 2008, I left behind my day-to-day duties with Galileo and took on the title Founder Emeritus. What a relief, a few months later, not to have to deal professionally with the housing crash that nearly wrecked America! Gary and Todd kept Galileo afloat, but they had a rough go of it for about three years.

Shannon and I decided to keep our penthouse on Fifth Avenue. We were city people, after all, and besides, we decided to situate the offices of the Brown Family Foundation in New York, in the Chrysler Building, just a few floors below Galileo. It gave me a way to stay in touch with Gary, and as founder emeritus of Galileo, I made sure I had the right to pop in anytime to use a Bloomberg terminal. This comes in handy as I manage the foundation's investments and our personal portfolio. I stay away from serious involvement with Galileo, but Gary and I still talk frequently about investment ideas.

I knew I wanted to start spending more time in Chicago. I could visit regularly with Mom, take in a few Cubs games, and even look in on the high school kids playing at the Galileo Capital Soccer Complex.

I convinced my mother to sell her house in Oak Park, and we built a large unit for her in the Aqua. We included a wing for ourselves with one of the most beautiful views of Lake Michigan in all of Chicago. As early owners, Shannon and I had our dinner with Jeanne Gang, and she has become one of our closest friends.

We also decided we liked Phoenix and other parts of Arizona well enough to spend more time there. We flew out regularly, and Mike always picked us up at Cutter.

I really liked the guy, and I elected to bankroll him in a small limo business all his own. Within a few years, he paid back the loan, and he had the largest limo service in Phoenix. He stopped driving, using his time instead to run the business and teach his drivers all about client care. He married Karina, and Shannon and I spend a few evenings drinking and dining with them whenever we head to the Valley.

I also became involved with Taliesin West. I never shook feeling bad about how much it had deteriorated, and it became one of the early recipients of a Brown Family Foundation grant. I wangled my way onto the board, and I asked RK Stewart to help us recruit the right architects to turn the operations around. My friends in Oak Park and New York like seeing me enhance the legacy of Frank Lloyd Wright. I made sure they received a behind-the-scenes tour when they came to Phoenix. I also make sure they prove their love of Wright by forking over a hefty donation to Taliesin West.

My mom comes to Phoenix with us in the winter. She's had enough of the Chicago deep freeze.

Jeff and Janis Fowler continue to live in the Valley. Needless to say, Fowler and I have never found a reason to visit with one another, but Janis, Shannon and my mom have lunch together once or twice a year. We've also had dinner a few times at Don Cunningham's home in Paradise Valley.

After a few years, we decided to build our own home in Phoenix. We had to tackle the question of where we wanted to live. We decided in 2011.

The Phoenix housing market had not come out of the tank, so as buyers, we definitely had an advantage. We thought about living downtown. Arizona State University keeps moving more of its classes there, and an influx of college students are making the area more lively. Some brave developers committed themselves to creating interesting residential options downtown. We nearly bought a condo right across the street from the west side of the Diamondbacks stadium.

But after several discussions, Shannon and I decided we wanted something different from our urban penthouse in Manhattan. We bought 10 acres at the northern edge of Scottsdale, right next to the McDowell Sonoran Preserve. We often hike the preserve's trails, which lets us roam among 30,000 acres of cactus, wildflowers, ducks, egrets and cormorants. It's a great winter refuge for us, far removed from the sometimes bone-chilling New York winters.

We chose Mary Goseyun, an Apache and a graduate of the Taliesin West architectural program, to design our house. Soon after I came on the board at Taliesin West, several professors raved to me about her work. She had a knack for taking Wright's Prairie style and reinterpreting it for the desert.

She gave us several options. The one we chose created a wall of windows on the north side of the house, which faces the preserve. This includes our bedroom. We have no concerns about privacy. No one will be building north of us, and we enjoy waking up to the Arizona landscape, which I've come to appreciate as harsh but beautiful.

Mary led the effort to make the house carbon neutral. We had all the resources we needed to try new technology, so she hooked us up with a solar system to keep us totally off the grid. We live so far out we have to truck in our own water to fill the small reservoir on our property. Not the most sustainable practice, I know, but compromises are part of life, right? And it has the virtue of making us really careful with how we use water. It would be a real pain to run out between deliveries, and I don't like the thought of paying for extra trips from the water truck.

For the most part, I gave Shannon a free hand to work with Mary on design, both interior and exterior. I had only one demand. I wanted copper to be used everywhere possible, in the wiring, the plumbing, the roof, and wherever it made sense in the interior design.

Copper, after all, brought us to Arizona, and it supercharged our bank account. I wanted our home to be a tribute to copper. And besides, I really love the look of the red metal.

About the Author

Peter Faur worked in St. Louis as a reporter and editor before making the transition to public relations in the early 1980s. His employers and clients have included corporate leaders in telecommunications, brewing, chemical manufacturing and copper mining. He holds master's degrees in journalism and business administration. Today he and his wife, Pat, live in Phoenix.

Made in the USA
San Bernardino, CA
30 March 2019